A LADY IN BLACK

A LADY IN BLACK

FLORENCE WARDEN

Originally published in 1895.
Published by Wildside Press.
wildsidepress.com

CHAPTER I.
A MYSTERY SOMEWHERE.

"AND besides, you know, my dear Mrs. Rose, there is generally something wrong about a woman who dresses so very well."

So spoke Mrs. Bonnington, the Vicar's wife, laying down the law; a law indeed, which most English women are ready to take for granted. Mrs. Rose, a tall, thin, pale lady who had "nerves," and who, on this bright April morning, wore a woollen shawl half off her shoulders as she sat in the warm sun by the dining-room window, assented readily.

"That's what I always say. Especially a widow. I'm sure if anything were to happen to my husband," went on Mrs. Rose euphemistically, "the last thing I should think about would be my dress. I should be far too unhappy to trouble myself about the fit of my dresses or the shape of my bonnets."

Now this was perhaps true, as Mrs. Rose, though she spent as much money and as much thought upon her clothes as her compeers, never succeeded in looking as if her clothes had been made for her, or as if the subject of "fit" were of any importance.

Mrs. Bonnington shook her head with vague disquietude, and resumed her homily.

"I assure you the matter has caused me a good deal of anxiety. You know how solicitous both the Vicar and I are about the tone of the parish."

"I do indeed," murmured Mrs. Rose sympathetically.

"You know how hard we work to keep up a high standard. Why, everybody knows that it was through us that those objectionable people at Colwyn Lodge went away, and how we would do anything to rid the place of those terrible Solomons at Stone Court!"

At the other end of the room, a young face, with gray eyes full of mischief, was turned in the direction of Mrs. Bonnington with a satirical smile. Mabin Rose, the overgrown, awkward step-daughter of Mrs. Rose, who hated the Vicar's wife, and called her a busybody and a gossip, brought her darning nearer to the table and dashed headlong into the fray.

"Papa wouldn't thank you if you did drive the Solomons out of the parish, as you did the people at Colwyn Lodge, Mrs. Bonnington," broke in the clear young voice that would be heard. "He says Mr. Solomon is the best tenant he ever had, and that he wishes that some of the Christians were like him."

"Hush, Mabin. Go on with your work, and don't interrupt with your rude remarks," said Mrs. Rose sharply. "I am quite sure your father never said such a thing, except perhaps in fun," she went on, turning apologetically to her visitor. "Nobody is more anxious about 'tone' and

1

all those things than Mr. Rose, and he was saying only yesterday that he would rather I didn't call upon this Mrs. Dale until something more was known about her."

Again the young face at the other end of the table looked up mutinously; but this time Mabin controlled her inclination to protest. She looked down again, and began to darn furiously, to the relief of her feelings, but to the injury of the stocking.

Mrs. Bonnington went on:

"You were quite right. It's not that I wish to be uncharitable."

"Of course not," assented Mrs. Rose with fervor.

"But a woman like yourself, with daughters to take care of, cannot be too careful. Young people are so easily led away; they think so much of the mere outside. They are so easily dazzled and taken in by appearances."

Mabin grew red, perceiving that this little sermon by the way was directed at herself. Her step-sisters, Emily and Ethel, one of whom could be heard "practising" in the drawing-room, were not the sort of girls to be led away by anything.

"But why shouldn't a nice face mean something nice?" put in the rash young woman again.

The fact was that Mabin had been charmed with the sweet pink-and-white face and blue eyes of Mrs. Dale, their new neighbor at "The Towers," and was mentally comparing the widow's childlike charms with the acidulated attractions of the Vicar's dowdy wife.

"And why," pursued Mabin, as both the elder ladies seemed to pause to gain strength to fall upon her together, "shouldn't she be just as sorry for her husband's death because she looks nice over it? It seemed to me, when she sat near us at church on Sunday, that she had the saddest face I had ever seen. And as for her corrupting us by her 'tone,' she won't have anything to do with any of us. Mrs. Warren has called upon her, and the Miss Bradleys and Mrs. Peak and a lot more people, and she's always 'not at home.' So even if she is wicked, I should think you might let her stay. Surely she can't do us much harm just by having her frocks better made than the rest of us."

When Mabin had finished this outrageous speech, there was an awful pause. Mrs. Rose hardly knew how to administer such a reproof as should be sufficiently scathing; while Mrs. Bonnington waited in solemn silence for the reproof to come. Mabin looked from her step-mother's face to that of the Vicar's wife, and thought she had better retire before the avalanche descended. So she gathered up her work hastily, running her darning-needle into her hand in her excitement, muttered an awkward apology and excuse for her disappearance at the same time, and shot out of the room in the ungainly way which had so often before caused her stepmother to shudder, as she did now.

When the door had closed upon the girl, closed, unfortunately, with a bang, Mrs. Bonnington sighed.

"I am afraid," she said, unconsciously assuming still more of her usual clerical tone and accent, "that Mabin must be a great anxiety to you!"

Mrs. Rose sighed and closed her eyes for a moment, wearily.

"If you could realize *how* great an anxiety," she murmured in a solemn tone, "you would pity me! If it were not that Mr. Rose gives his authority to support mine in dealing with her, she would be absolutely unmanageable, I assure you."

"A froward spirit! And one singularly unsusceptible to good influences," said the Vicar's wife. "However, we must persevere with her, and hope for a future blessing on our labors, even if it should come too late for us to be witnesses of her regeneration."

"I am sure I have always done my best for her, and treated her just as I have my own children. But you see with what different results! The seed is the same, but the soil is not. I don't know whether you knew her mother? But I suppose Mabin must take after her. She is utterly unlike her father."

"She is indeed. Mr. Rose is such a particularly judicious, upright man. The Vicar has the highest respect for him."

Mrs. Bonnington paused, to give full effect to this noble encomium. Mrs. Rose acknowledged it by a graceful bend of the head, and went on:

"The great failing about poor Mabin is that she is not womanly. And that is the one thing above all that my husband asks of a woman. Let her only be womanly, he always says, and I will forgive everything else. Now my own girls are that, above everything."

"Ah!" exclaimed Mrs. Bonnington with decision; "but that is just the fault of our age, Mrs. Rose. Girls are no longer brought up to be contented to be girls. They must put themselves on the same footing with their brothers. Mabin is in the fashion. And no doubt that is all she desires. You see how this Mrs. Dale has caught hold of her imagination, by nothing but her fashionable clothes!"

Mrs. Rose put on a womanly air of absolute helplessness:

"Well, what can I do?" said she.

Mrs. Bonnington came a little nearer.

"In the case of this Mrs. Dale," said she in a lower voice, "go on just as you have begun. Do not call upon her. Do not have anything to do with her. To tell you the truth, it was about her that I came to see you this morning. She has already brought mischief into our own peaceful home. She is a dangerous woman."

"Dear me! You don't mean that!" said Mrs. Rose with vivid interest.

3

"Unhappily I do. My son Rudolph came back from his ship only ten days ago, and already he can think of nothing but this Mrs. Dale."

"After having had the unpardonable insolence to leave your call unreturned, she has got hold of your son?" gasped Mrs. Rose.

"Well, not exactly that, as far as I know," admitted the Vicar's wife. "He says he has never spoken to her. And the dear boy has never told me an untruth before."

"But if this dreadful woman has entangled him, of course she might make him say anything!" cried Mrs. Rose in sympathetic agonies.

"I should not like to accuse a fellow-woman of doing that," replied Mrs. Bonnington, severely; "but I think it is a bad and unnatural sign, when my son, who has never taken the least notice of any of the young girls in the neighborhood, becomes absorbed, in a few days, in the doings of a person who is a complete stranger to him and who calls herself a widow."

"Then don't you think," purred Mrs. Rose, with the eagerness of one who scents a scandal, "that she *is* a widow?"

There was a pause. And Mrs. Bonnington spoke next, with the deliberation of one who has a great duty to perform.

"I should be very sorry to have it said of me that I was the first to start a rumor which might be thought unchristian or unkind," she said with a deprecatory wave of the brown cotton gloves she wore in the mornings. "But I have thought it my duty to make inquiries, and I deeply regret to say that I have found out several things which lead me to the conclusion that this person has settled down in our midst under false pretences."

"You don't say so!"

"You shall judge for yourself. In the first place, although she calls herself Mrs. Dale, the initials on some of her linen are 'D. M.' Now M. does not stand for 'Dale,' does it?"

"Perhaps her maiden name began with M.," suggested Mrs. Rose.

"My informant tells me," went on Mrs. Bonnington, as if offended by the interruption, "that in her old books, school-books and work of that sort, there is written the name 'Dorothy Leatham.' So that she seems to have passed already by three different names. I leave it to your own common sense whether that is not a curious circumstance, considering that she is still young."

"It is certainly curious, very curious. And—and—"

Mrs. Rose hardly liked to ask on what authority her visitor made these statements, which savored strongly of the back-stairs. She had hardly paused an instant before Mrs. Bonnington rushed into further details:

"And now here is another thing which is very strange: her servants have none of them been with her long. They were all engaged together, three months ago in London, not by Mrs. Dale herself, but by an old lady whose name nobody seems to know. Now isn't that rather remarkable? They all came down here, and had the place ready for their mistress, before they so much as saw her."

Mrs. Bonnington leaned back in her chair, and drew on her brown cotton gloves further. Mrs. Rose wondered again as to the source of this information. She felt a little ashamed of listening to all this gossip, and was less inclined than her friend to take a suspicious view of the case, strange though it was. So she contented herself with murmured interjections, to fill up the pause before Mrs. Bonnington went on again:

"However, I have got a clew to where she came from, for a van-load of furniture came down before she arrived, and it came from Todcaster."

"Todcaster!" echoed Mrs. Rose. "Then we shall soon know something more about her. Mr. Rose's old friend, Mrs. Haybrow, is coming down to see us early next month. She lived near Todcaster when she was a girl, and she often goes back to the old place, and keeps in touch with all the people about there."

"Well," said Mrs. Bonnington, rising from her chair, and speaking in a rather more stilted tone than at first, with the consciousness that her news had hardly been received as she had expected, "I sincerely trust we may find we have been mistaken. No one will rejoice more unfeignedly than I if she proves to be indeed what she gives herself out to be. Indeed, if she had received me frankly at the outset, I would have shown her such Christian sympathy as one soul can give to another without asking any questions. And it is only in the interests of our young people that I lift up my voice now."

The Vicar's wife then took her leave, and went on her way to complete her morning rounds. She was rather a terrible person, this little, faded middle-aged woman with the curate's voice and the curate's manner, uniting, as she did, a desperate interest in other people's affairs with a profound conviction that her interference in them could only be for good. But she had her good points. A devoted, submissive, and worshipful wife, she modified her worship by considering herself the Vicar's guardian angel. A parish busybody and tyrant, she never spared herself and could show true womanly kindness to such of her husband's parishioners as were not of "a froward spirit."

Unluckily, she had not the power of conciliating, but had, on the contrary, a grand talent for raising up antagonism in unregenerate minds like those of the unfortunate Mabin.

The young girl had been both sorry and ashamed at her own loss of temper. Not that an outburst such as that she had indulged in was any unusual thing. Like many young girls of spirit under injudicious rule,

Mabin was in a state of perpetual friction with those around her. Her step-mother was not intentionally unkind; but poor Mabin had to suffer from the constant comparison of her unruly and independent self with her quiet and insipid half-sisters.

And the worst of it was that her father was even less indulgent than his wife to her waywardness. A stiff, straight-laced, narrow-minded man, accustomed to be looked up to and deferred to by the female members of his household, he disapproved in the strongest manner both of the erratic moods of his eldest daughter, and of her longing for independence. It was from him, indeed, that Mabin chiefly suffered. She looked upon the cold, handsome, aquiline face of her father with something very much like horror, and the mere fact that he approved only of submissive "womanly" women seemed to goad her into the very rebelliousness and independence which shocked him so deeply.

At the same time that he disapproved of her, however, Mr. Rose did not hesitate to avail himself of his daughter's bright wits; and if any task requiring a little thought or a little judgment presented itself, it was always upon Mabin's shoulders that he put the burden.

He had even gone so far, protesting loudly the while against the "unfeminine" practice, as to allow Mabin to ride a bicycle; and it was on this machine that the girl was expected to go into Seagate two or three times a week, to fetch him his books and magazines from the local library.

As Mrs. Bonnington descended the steps of the big stone house, and, emerging from the portico, made her way down the broad gravel path to the gate, she met Mabin coming out by the side gate among the evergreens with her bicycle by her side.

Now if there was one thing more detestable in the eyes of the Vicar's wife than another, it was a bicycle. But this detestation increased tenfold when the rider of the obnoxious machine was a woman. It was her one grievance against upright Mr. Rose that he allowed his nineteen-year-old daughter to "career about the country" on the abominable thing.

She uttered an involuntary "Ugh!" of disgust as the thing almost touched her uplifted skirts.

"I beg your pardon. I hope I didn't run against you. I am so clumsy," said Mabin with studied politeness.

"You can't expect to be anything but clumsy while you use such a thing as that!" said Mrs. Bonnington severely. "I wish for your own sake it would get broken, that you might never be seen in an attitude so unbecoming to a gentlewoman again."

"Is it you who tell your sons to throw stones at it when I am riding past the Vicarage?" said Mabin, trying to speak civilly, while the blood rose to her cheeks. "Walter struck the hind wheel two days ago, and now I have to walk as long as I am within stone's-throw of your garden wall."

"I have heard nothing about it," said Mrs. Bonnington icily.

"Of course you wouldn't," said Mabin, keeping her tone in check. "But I see Rudolph has taken to riding one too since he's been back. So if they throw stones at me, I can have my revenge upon him," she concluded darkly.

"If girls unsex themselves, they can't expect to be treated with the chivalry they used to receive," said Mrs. Bonnington, as, not caring to continue the encounter with the rebellious one, she turned her back, and went down the hill.

CHAPTER II.
A PENITENT.

MABIN looked at Mrs. Bonnington's retreating figure, half regretfully and half resentfully. The regret was for her own incivility; the resentment was for the want of tact which had provoked it.

Mabin, like so many other young girls on the threshold of womanhood, lived in a constant state of warfare both with herself and her neighbors. Sensitive, affectionate, hasty tempered and wilful, she was at the same time almost morbidly modest and mistrustful of herself; so that she passed her time in alternate bursts of angry resentment against those who misunderstood her, and fits of remorse for her own shortcomings.

She now mounted her bicycle with the feeling that the Vicar's wife had spoilt her morning's ride for her. Not by any means a vain girl, she underrated her own attractions, which included a pretty, gray-eyed little flower-face, a fair skin, and short, soft, dark-brown hair. But she was keenly alive to the reproach of clumsiness, which had so often been cast at her. She had shot up, within the last three years, to a height which, together with the girlish leanness of her figure, had caused her to be called, even outside the family circle, "a lamp-post" and a "gawky creature." And although she stubbornly refused to take to the long skirts which would have lent her the grace she wanted, she nourished a smouldering indignation against her traducers.

And chief among these were the boys of the Vicarage, against whom, as against their mother for her criticisms, and their father for his dull sermons, her spirit was always in arms.

The strife between the Bonningtons and the Roses had not always been so keen. Indeed, in the old days when they were children together, Mabin and Rudolph had got on well enough together, and had exchanged love-tokens of ends of slate pencil, lumps of chalk, and bird's eggs. But with advancing years had come first coolness and then estrangement. So that it was now the correct thing among the Bonnington boys to laugh at Mabin for being "advanced," "superior," "a New Woman," and a "fright;" while she, on her side, treated them with lofty contempt as "savages" and "boors."

Mabin had not gone twenty yards, however, on her way up the slight ascent, when she saw something which diverted her thoughts from the Vicarage people. The gates at "The Towers" were wide open, and Mrs. Dale's smart victoria, with its well-matched pair of small, dark-brown horses, came out so suddenly that Mabin had to jump off her bicycle to avoid a collision. Alone in the carriage sat a lady in deep mourning, who turned and looked out anxiously at the girl, and stopped the carriage to speak to her.

"I'm so sorry! I hope you didn't hurt yourself, in having to jump off so quickly?" asked the lady in black, in a sweet, plaintive voice that struck some chord in Mabin's heart, and made the girl gasp, and pause before she could answer.

"Oh no, oh no, thank you. One often has to do that," stammered the girl, flushing, and speaking with a shy constraint which made her tone cold and almost rude.

And she knew it, poor child, and was miserable over it; miserable to think that now when she had an opportunity of speaking to the being who had excited in her an enthusiastic admiration, she was throwing her chance away.

A common and a most tragic experience with most young girls.

One thing, however, Mabin was able to do. In the shy look with which she returned Mrs. Dale's kind gaze of inquiry, she took in a picture of a lovely woman which remained impressed on her mind ineffaceably.

Mrs. Dale was a lovely woman, lovelier than Mabin had thought when she only got glimpses of the lady's profile from her seat in church, or peeps at her through a thick black veil. Mrs. Dale wore a black veil to-day, but in the open carriage, in the full glare of the sun, her beauty was evident enough.

A little woman, plump, pink, childlike in face and figure, with wavy fair hair, infantine blue eyes, and a red-lipped mouth which was all the more lovable, more attractive for not being on the strict lines of beauty, Mrs. Dale had, so Mabin felt, exactly the right features and the right expression for the sweet voice she had just heard. And through the beauty, and through the voice, the girl, inspired perhaps by the mourning dress, thought she detected a sadness which seemed to her the most pathetic thing in the world.

In two moments the interview was over; Mrs. Dale had smiled upon her sweetly, bidden her farewell merely with a bend of her head, and driven away, leaving Mabin to scold herself for her idiocy in throwing away an opportunity which she might never have again.

She did not try to overtake the carriage; she watched it down the open road, until the shining coil of silky fair hair under the black crape bonnet grew dim in the distance. And then, with a shrug of her shoulders and a murmur that "it was just like her," Mabin turned defiantly into the road which led past the Vicarage.

However, nobody was about to throw stones at the bicycle on this occasion; and it was not until she had reached Seagate, changed her father's books at the library, and matched a skein of cable silk for Emily, that she was reminded afresh of the existence of the Bonningtons by the sight of Rudolph, in his knickerbockers and gaiters, standing by his bicycle while he lit a cigarette.

Unconsciously Mabin frowned a little. And unluckily Rudolph saw the frown. She meant to pass him without appearing to notice him, but he foresaw the intention, and was nettled by it. For Rudolph, with his black eyes and curly black hair, and his sunbrowned face, was the handsomest fellow in the neighborhood when he was on shore, and was accustomed to a great deal of kindness and civility from Mabin's sex. Her rudeness, which arose more from shyness than from the lofty contempt he supposed, puzzled the young fellow, and made him angry. He remembered their ancient comradeship, which she seemed to have forgotten; and most unwisely he let a spirit of "devilment" get the better of him, and addressed her as if they had been still on the old terms.

"Good-morning, Mabin," said he.

She gave him a bend of the head, without looking at him, and was passing on to the place where her bicycle stood outside the door of a shop. But he would not let her escape so.

"Mayn't I offer you a cigarette?"

To do him justice Rudolph had not noticed that a small boy with a basket stood near enough to hear. The boy burst into shrill laughter, and Mabin turned fiercely. For once she did not stoop.

"I'm afraid you have forgotten a great deal since you went to sea," she said in a voice which she could not keep steady.

The young man was surprised, and rather shocked at the way in which he had been received. He had been anxious to heal the breach between her and himself, and he had thought that a dash into their old familiarity might avail where more carefully studied attempts had failed.

Before he could do more than begin to apologize, to appeal to their old friendship, Mabin had got on her bicycle and ridden away.

The sun was beating down fiercely by this time upon the white chalky roads; but Mabin rode on recklessly, at a higher speed than usual. She was well on her way back to Stone, when, turning her head to look along the road she had come by, she perceived that Rudolph was not far behind. She had forgiven his indiscretion by this time, and rather hoped that he was following quickly on purpose to "make it up." So she went on her way through a group of straggling cottages, at a rather slower pace.

There was a sharp bend in the road at this point, and just as she sounded her bell in turning the corner, she saw Rudolph, who was now close behind, dismount and pick something up from the road. The next moment something struck the front wheel of her bicycle, and she and her machine were flung with violence down in the road.

She had time to utter a cry, no more, before the crash came.

Then she remembered nothing, knew nothing, until she heard somebody sobbing close to her ears; and opening her eyes, she saw the sweet face of Mrs. Dale, with the black veil thrown back, and with tears in the blue eyes, leaning over her tenderly.

Mrs. Dale uttered a cry of joy, and another voice, which Mabin recognized as Rudolph's, said: "Thank God! she isn't dead, at any rate."

"Are you better, dear? Are you in any pain?" asked Mrs. Dale with so much solicitude that answering tears of sympathetic emotion started into the girl's own eyes.

"I am quite well, quite well," said Mabin. "Only—only—I think my foot hurts."

Rudolph and Mrs. Dale exchanged glances.

"I thought so," said he. "She's broken her ankle."

Mrs. Dale's pretty eyes began to fill again.

"We must lift her into the carriage," said she. "And you will go on and prepare her mother, and see that a doctor is sent for at once."

And, in spite of the protests she feebly made, Mabin was gently raised from the ground by Rudolph's strong arms, and helped into the victoria, where Mrs. Dale took her seat, and, telling the coachman to drive slowly, insisted on making her own plump little shoulder the pillow for the girl's head.

But Mabin, having recovered her spirits, if not her walking powers, wanted to talk to the new friend she had so unexpectedly made.

"You are very good to me," she said. "I have never had so much kindness from any one since my mother died. It was so strange; when I woke up just now I felt what I thought was my mother's touch again. And yet I had forgotten all about that. For she has been dead fifteen years."

"Poor child!" said Mrs. Dale. "I am glad of that, dear, that I reminded you of her," she whispered gently.

"Of course I don't mean that," went on Mabin quickly, trying to sit up. "I don't mean that you could be a mother to me now, as I am. That does sound ridiculous! You couldn't be my mother when you are the same age as myself."

As a matter of fact, Mabin looked older than her companion. But when the conversation thus turned to herself, Mrs. Dale's pink face grew suddenly pale, and Mabin looked at her shyly, and flushed, feeling that she had said something wrong. But almost before she was conscious that she had touched some sensitive spot, Mrs. Dale said softly:

"Go on talking, dear, about your mother, or—or anything. I am lonely, you know; very lonely. And it is a treat to hear you talk."

The girl flushed again, this time with surprise.

"You like to hear me talk! Ah, then you must be lonely indeed. For they say at home I never talk without saying the very last thing I ought to say."

As she came to the end of her speech, Mabin found that her words insensibly began to run the one into the other, and that her voice died away. And, greatly to her own astonishment, she found her head falling heavily upon that of her new friend.

"Ah, child, it is selfish of me to make you talk!" cried Mrs. Dale. "You are faint, and must rest now. Come and talk to me some other time."

Mabin overcame the faintness which had seized her, and quite suddenly raised her head again. The little excitement of the hope held out to her brought all her senses back.

"Come and see you! Oh, may I? I should like to so much!"

The girl almost nestled, as she spoke, against her new friend.

But over Mrs. Dale's fair, childlike face there came at once a sort of shadow, as if a terrible remembrance had suddenly taken the power for all pleasurable emotion from her. It almost seemed to Mabin that the little hands made a movement as if to push her away.

And then there burst forth from the infantile red lips some words which struck terror into her young hearer, so bitter, so full of sadness, of biting remorse, were they:

"No, child, no. You must not come. *I am too wicked!*"

The girl was struck dumb. She wanted to comfort pretty Mrs. Dale; she wanted to laugh at her self-accusation, to express incredulity, amusement. But in the face of that look of anguish, of that inexpressibly mournful cry straight from the heart, she could not even open her lips. She knew that there was some grief here which no words of comfort could touch.

So deeply absorbed was she in the silent compassion which kept her with lowered eyelids and mute lips, that she was quite startled when Mrs. Dale's voice, speaking in her ordinary tones, struck again upon her ear.

"That young fellow who picked you up is one of the Vicar's sons, isn't he?"

"Yes," answered Mabin in a rather colder voice.

"He seems a very nice lad, and very much interested in—somebody?" suggested Mrs. Dale archly.

Mabin laughed.

"Yes, so he is. But it is not the 'somebody' you mean," answered she. "Mrs. Bonnington, that's his mother, says he can think about nothing but—Mrs. Dale!"

Again the sweet face changed; and it was in a low voice full of sadness that the lady in black said, slowly and deliberately:

"I hope with all my heart that she has made a mistake." Then, with a rapid gesture, as if brushing away some thought which was full of untold

12

terror, she added with a shudder: "Don't let us talk about it. It is too horrible!"

CHAPTER III.
AN INVITATION AND A WARNING.

MABIN's sprained ankle was a more serious affair than she had supposed. For a month she never left the house, and for another she went out in a wheel-chair, or hopped about on a pair of crutches.

And during all that time she caught no glimpse of the pretty neighbor who had done her such eminent service at the time of the accident. In vain she had hung about the road outside "The Towers" looking up at the west side of the house, which was built into the wall alongside the road, trying to distinguish the fair, blue-eyed face at one of the windows which peeped sombrely out of the ivy.

Dreary the place looked, Mabin thought, as she pondered over the mystery surrounding the lady in black. The lowest window visible from the road was about three feet above the girl's head; and all she could see was a pair of crimson moreen curtains, which, she thought, harmonized ill with what she had seen of the tenant of the gloomy house. The house had long been "To let, Furnished." But why had not dainty Mrs. Dale improved away those curtains?

Mabin did not usually trouble her head about such trifles as furniture; but she had enshrouded the figure of the pretty widow in romance; and she felt that her fairy queen was not living up to her proper standard in contenting herself with crimson moreen.

"What are you looking at so intently?"

Mabin, who, leaning on her crutches, was gazing up at that mysteriously interesting window, started violently as she saw a white hand, glistening with diamonds, thrust suddenly out through the ivy in the midst of a space which she had taken for blank wall.

And, parting the close-growing branches, Mrs. Dale peeped out, pink and fair and smiling, from a window at the same level as the one Mabin had been watching, but so thickly covered with ivy that the girl had not suspected its existence.

"I—I was looking for you. I was hoping to see you," stammered Mabin.

"And now that you have seen me, won't you please condescend to see a little more of me?" asked Mrs. Dale. "I won't eat you up if you come into my den. Look, here is another inhabitant whom I have entrapped. But there are strawberries enough for three."

Mabin hesitated; not from any scruples about the propriety of visiting the lady about whom so much gossip was talked, certainly, but because she was shy, and because the thought of a meeting and a talk with her ideal heroine and a stranger seemed rather formidable.

But Mrs. Dale would not allow her time to refuse.

"I will send the other inhabitant down to let you in," said she.

And the ivy closed again, and Mabin could hear the lady's voice giving some directions to some person within. She moved mechanically, on her crutches, toward the high closed gates. And by the time she reached them they were opening, and Rudolph was holding them back for her.

The girl could not repress a slight exclamation of astonishment. Rudolph reddened.

"You are surprised to see me," said he, rather bashfully. "I hope you won't refuse to come in because I am here? I will go away rather than that."

Mabin hesitated. She was not very worldly-wise, but it seemed to her that there was something rather strange about his presence in the house where the rest of the Vicar's family were not allowed to enter. And at the same moment she remembered Mrs. Dale's apparent horror at the idea of the young fellow's admiration for her.

Rudolph's color deepened still more.

"Why are you always so rude to me, Mabin, or I suppose I ought to say—Miss Rose?" asked he quickly. "Doesn't it seem rather unfair, when you come to think of it? We were great chums once, you know? Weren't we?"

"When we were children, yes," replied Mabin stiffly.

"And why not now?"

The blood rushed to the girl's forehead.

"How can you ask?" she said, indignantly. "When I owe my lameness to you?"

Rudolph stared at her, as if uncertain whether he heard aright.

"To me?"

"Why, yes. Surely you don't pretend it was not you who threw the stone which knocked my bicycle over?"

The stiff haughtiness with which she said this melted suddenly into apologetic alarm when she saw by the change to fierce indignation in Rudolph that she had made another, and most absurd blunder. At first he could only stare at her in speechless anger and amazement.

"Do you take me for a street-urchin?" he asked at last.

Mabin recovered herself a little, and refused to be withered up. "Your brothers do it," she said below her breath.

"Then I'll give the little beggars a good hiding the first time I catch them at it," said Rudolph sharply. "But I should have thought you could distinguish the difference between a man and a schoolboy, and not have visited their sins upon me."

15

Mabin felt miserable. She blushed, she stammered when she tried to speak; and the tears came into her eyes.

"I—I'm sorry!" she said in a constrained voice. "I—I see, I might have known. But you know—you were rude to me—that very day—when I saw you at Seagate!"

"Ah! I remember! I asked you to have a cigarette. It was injudicious, not rude. You should have made a distinction again."

There was an awkward silence. Rudolph was still resentful; but when he saw the downcast eyes, and the tears which were beginning to fringe the long black lashes, he found himself softening. And, putting her hand too hastily into her pocket for the handkerchief to wipe away her tears, Mabin dropped one of her crutches.

"Let me help you along," said he in a gentle voice, as he picked up the fallen crutch. "I don't like to see a girl using those things."

And, without waiting for her permission, he thrust the crutch under one arm, and insisted on supporting the unwilling girl with the other. And as they crossed the broad gravelled space to the portico, in the shade of the trees, Mabin felt a curious sensation of peace and of pleasure, and suddenly looked up at her companion with a frank smile.

"I'm very glad we're friends again," said she.

And he, smiling too, but with a little more malice, a little more guile, than she, answered readily:

"Why, so am I. But I must remind you that it is your fault, not mine, that we have ever been anything else."

Mabin hung her head, feeling rather guilty, but with yet more enjoyment of the present reconciliation than remorse for the past estrangement. Instead of taking her straight in, Rudolph led her across the gravel to a flower-border, where, in a little open patch of sunlight, a rosebush grew. It was a "Mrs. John Lang," and the huge pink blossoms were in their full beauty and fragrance.

"I've brought you here," he said didactically, "to read you a moral lesson. Here we have a rose, full of beauty and sweetness to every one, but without any thorns. While *some* Roses I know——"

"Are all thorns to everybody, and are without any beauty," finished Mabin for him, laughing, "and without any sweetness."

"No, no, not at all. But they seldom let you come near enough to admire the beauty, and they are rather chary of their sweetness. Now I hope you'll profit by this lesson."

"To be sure I—shan't!" replied Mabin with a rather doleful smile. "I do try to be less—less objectionable—sometimes," she added with seriousness which made Rudolph smile. "But it doesn't seem to be very successful. I think I'm going to give up the effort and accept the fate of 'an awful example' as serenely as I can."

Rudolph tried not to let his smile grow too broad for politeness.

"You are an odd girl," he said at last. "Or is it another insult to tell you so?"

Mabin shook her head.

"If it's an insult," answered she, "it is one that I'm used to."

"One is almost as much afraid of saying anything complimentary to you as of giving you what you call insults," he began cautiously. "Otherwise I would tell you that I like 'odd' people, people who don't always say and do the right thing, that is."

"Then you ought to appreciate me," retorted Mabin quickly. "For everybody says I always do and say the *wrong* thing!"

"I do appreciate you."

Mabin laughed and blushed.

"I only said that in fun," she said awkwardly.

"Well, I said what I did in earnest."

"Mrs. Dale will be wondering what has become of us," said Mabin.

She was not at all anxious to go in; but the pleasure she felt in this talk with Rudolph had grown rather alarming to her reserve. She began to fear that she would spoil it all by one of her far-famed blunders of speech. And so she chose to cut short the enjoyment while it could remain a recollection of unalloyed delight.

Rudolph, on his side, was in no hurry to go in; although he took a step obediently toward the portico.

From a feeling of perversity which she could not have accounted for, Mabin chose to talk about Mrs. Dale as they went slowly toward the house.

"I have been longing to see her ever since my accident," she said. "But although I have been always hovering about the place, wishing she would come out, to-day is the very first time I have caught sight of her."

"That is exactly my own experience," said Rudolph. "She seems to have given up driving about the place, and to have shut herself up in this dreary old house just like a nun."

"Oh!" said Mabin, feeling quite relieved to hear that he had not, as she had supposed, been in the society of the beautiful widow constantly since the day of the accident.

"Yes," he went on. "I was passing by only half an hour ago, when I glanced up at the windows, and Mrs. Dale stopped me to ask if I had heard how you were. And then she asked me in, saying she felt lonely. And so should I, so would any one, in that mouldy old house all alone."

"Poor lady! I am so sorry for her!" said Mabin.

Rudolph looked at her quickly.

"Do you feel like that about her too?" said he earnestly. "All the other people one meets are either jealous of her beauty, or envious of her handsome turnout, or angry with her for not wanting to make their acquaintance."

"I am very sorry for her," answered the girl gravely. "I feel certain that she has had some very great sorrow—"

"Why, yes, her husband's death," suggested Rudolph.

"Oh, yes, that of course," assented Mabin, surprised to find that the universal doubts whether Mrs. Dale really was a widow had infected her also. "But something even more than that, I should think. I have an idea that there is something tragic in her story, if one only knew it."

Rudolph said nothing to this, but he looked at his companion with a quick glance of surprise, as if he himself shared her opinion, and was astonished to find it echoed.

They were under the portico now, and as their footsteps sounded on the stone, they saw through the open door into the dark hall and heard Mrs. Dale's soft voice calling to them.

"It takes ever so much longer to get a thing done than to do it one's self!" she exclaimed brightly, with a sigh, as she came out of the room on the left, and invited them to go in. "I could have brought Miss Rose in in half the time, even if she had fought to get away. Did she fight?" went on Mrs. Dale with arch innocence.

They were in the room by this time, and Mabin, coming in out of the glare of the sun, stood for a few seconds without seeing anything. Then her hands were gently taken, and she found herself pushed into a low chair.

"Bring her some strawberries, Mr. Bonnington," said Mrs. Dale. "By the by, I may as well remark that I don't intend to call you Mr. Bonnington very long. I shall drop into plain 'Rudolph' very soon, if only to give a fresh shock to the neighborhood, to whom I am Shocker in ordinary."

"The sooner the better. I can't understand anybody's being Mr. Bonnington but my father. Now he looks equal to the dignity, while I don't. I always feel that there is a syllable too many for me, and that people despise me in consequence."

Mabin, who had recovered the use of her eyes, felt rather envious. The quick give and take of light talk like this was so different from the solemn conversations carried on at home, where her father laid down the law and everybody else agreed with him, that she felt this levity, while pleasant and amusing, to be something which would have caused the good folk at home to look askance.

18

"And how have you been, child, since that unhappy day when I saw you last?"

And Mrs. Dale came to the next chair, and piled sugar on the strawberries.

"Oh, I've been getting on all right, but it is tiresome not to be able to walk without those things. And it has made me in everybody's way," sighed Mabin.

"How is that?"

"Papa could have let the house to go abroad, as he wanted to, when the accident happened. Only I couldn't well be moved then. And now that I could go, he has lost the house he had heard of at Geneva, and one which he could have now is too small for us. So that I feel I am in the way again."

"Do you mean," asked Mrs. Dale quite eagerly, "that they could go if only they could dispose of you?"

"Yes. There is one room short."

Little Mrs. Dale sprang up, and the color in her cheeks grew pinker.

"Do you think," she asked, after a moment's pause, "that your parents would allow you to stay with me? If you would come?" she finished with a plaintive note of entreaty on the last words.

"Oh, I am sure they would, and I am sure I would!" cried Mabin, with undisguised delight.

And then quite suddenly the face of the black-robed lady grew ashy gray, and she sank down into her chair trembling from head to foot.

"No. I—I mustn't ask you," she said hoarsely.

And there was a silence, during which both her young hearers cast down their eyes, feeling that they dared not look at her. It was Mabin who spoke first. Putting her hand between the two white hands of Mrs. Dale, she said gently:

"Is it because you are lonely you want me to come?"

She did venture to look up then, startled by the shiver which convulsed Mrs. Dale as she spoke. And in the blue eyes she saw a look of terror which she never forgot.

"Lonely! Oh, child, you will never know how lonely!" burst from her pale lips.

"Then I will come," said Mabin. "I should like to come."

There was another silence. Mrs. Dale had evidently to put strong constraint upon herself to check an outburst of emotional gratitude. Rudolph, moved himself by the little scene, was looking out of the window. The lady in black presently spoke again, very gravely:

"I don't think you will be very much bored, dear, and you will be doing a great kindness to a fellow-creature. And yet—I hardly like—I don't feel that I ought——"

"But I feel that I must and shall," said Mabin brightly. "You don't know how beautiful it would be for me to feel that at last, for a little while, I shouldn't be in the way!"

And the overgrown girl, who was snubbed at home, had tears in her eyes at the remembrance of the kind touch which she had felt on the day of her accident. Mrs. Dale was too much moved to say much more, but it was agreed between the ladies that the suggestion should be formally made by the tenant of "The Towers" to the heads of the household at "Stone House" without delay, that Mabin should stay with her new friend during the absence abroad of the rest of the Rose family.

Mabin did notice, while they talked, that Rudolph remained not only silent but somewhat constrained; but it was not until she took her leave of Mrs. Dale, and he followed her out, that the young girl attached any importance to his reserve.

Once out of hearing of Mrs. Dale, who stood on the stone steps to bid them good-by, Rudolph asked her abruptly:

"Do you think they'll let you come?"

"Oh, yes, they'll only be too glad to get rid of me. Why do you ask in that tone?"

"Well, there is something I think I ought to tell you, if you are thinking of staying with Mrs. Dale."

"Well, what is it?"

"It is that she is being watched."

"Watched!"

"Yes, by a stranger, a man whom I have never seen in the place before. He hovers about this place, keeping out of range of possible eyes in the house, at all hours of the day and even of the night."

"But how do you know this?"

The words slipped out of her mouth, and it was not until she saw Rudolph redden that she saw that she was too inquisitive.

"I am sure of what I say, anyhow," said he quietly.

Mabin looked thoughtful.

"I don't care!" she said at last.

"I thought you wouldn't."

"And I shan't tell anybody anything about it."

"I was sure you wouldn't."

"But I shall tell Mrs. Dale."

Rudolph stopped and looked at her.

"I think you had better not do that," he said.

"But why should a person watch her, except with the intention of trying to do her some harm?"

"Well, I don't know. But I think if you do tell her, knowing how highly nervous she is, you will do her more harm than ever the mysterious watcher would. Perhaps you would even drive her out of the place, in which case most assuredly the watcher would go after her, while if we keep her here perhaps we may manage to draw his fangs."

Mabin felt frightened. Then, being a matter-of-fact girl, she got the better of this feeling quickly, and looked up keenly at her companion.

"What do you exactly mean by that?" she asked.

"Only that I will get hold of the man quietly and find out what his little game is. Though I can guess."

"Well, you can tell me what your guess is?"

"Why, debt, of course. One can see she is inclined to be extravagant, and very likely she has run up bills somewhere. Don't you think that seems likely?"

His tone was rather anxious, Mabin thought. But she answered indignantly:

"No, I don't. It would be very dishonorable to run away without paying one's debts, and I don't think you much of a friend to poor Mrs. Dale to suggest such a thing!"

Rudolph looked not guilty, but grave.

"Well" said he, "people don't hang about a place, at the risk of getting taken up 'on suspicion of loitering, for the purpose of committing a felony,' without some reason."

"Why," cried Mabin triumphantly, "that *is* the reason! Mrs. Dale has some lovely diamond rings, and the loitering gentleman wants to steal them!"

"Well, perhaps you are right," said Rudolph doubtfully.

"I am sure of it!" retorted Mabin resolutely. And she held out her hand. "Good-by, and thank you for your help."

"And you will remember my parable about the Roses?" said he, as he took her hand and thought he liked gray eyes after all better than blue ones.

"Perhaps," said Mabin cautiously, as she hopped away on her crutches.

CHAPTER IV.
WAS IT A RECOGNITION?

WHILE Mabin was still talking to Rudolph in the road between "The Towers" and "Stone House," a tall parlormaid, in snow-white French cap and ends, passed them, on her way from the former to the latter house, bearing a letter in her hand.

And when Mabin reached home, she found that the Powers had already received Mrs. Dale's invitation to Mabin.

In truth it had put both husband and wife into a position of some difficulty. For while, on the one hand, they were delighted at this opportunity of getting "the one too many" off their hands for a time, yet there were the opinions of their neighbors to be considered; and the tide of public feeling had set in strongly against the lady in black.

If her hair had been dark instead of fair, it would have made all the difference. The beauty which goes with brown hair and a more or less dark complexion is not so startling, not so sensational, as the loveliness of pink and white and gold which made Mrs. Dale so conspicuous. If again, she had not been in mourning, and such pretty mourning, they would have been readier to make allowance for her eccentricities. But the knowing ones had begun to discover that there were discrepancies in her attire, that her mourning was either too deep for diamond rings to be permissible, or not deep enough for the heavy black veil she wore.

So that, in short, it was now almost universally admitted that this person with the too showy carriage and horses, and the dangerously pretty face, was an individual to be avoided, and it was decided that her reluctance to enter the best society of the place, when that society had held out its uninviting arms to her, arose from a wholesome fear that the wise women of the place would "find her out."

Mr. Rose read Mrs. Dale's note twice through, very slowly, as if trying to discover hidden meanings in its simple words. Then he looked at his wife, who was watching him rather anxiously.

"Well, my dear, and what do you think?" asked he.

It pleased him to ask her opinion thus on most things, not that he ever had any intention of heeding her wishes in preference to his own, but in the hope that she would express some modest inclination one way or the other, to give him an impetus in the opposite direction.

"I think, dear, that it would hardly do," murmured the lady, hoping that for once her husband would fall in with her views. "You must have heard the way in which people talk about this Mrs. Dale, so that it would be thought very strange if we let Mabin stay with her. Don't you think it was rather underhand of her to get hold of the child this afternoon?"

"Underhand! Certainly not," replied Mr. Rose with decision. "The most natural thing in the world, considering how kind she was to the girl at the time of her accident. And as for the talk of the place, why, if you listened to all the old women say you would never go outside your door for fear your neighbors should think you were going to steal their hens!"

There was a pause. She would not irritate him by another remark. So he presently went on:

"I suppose you think the Vicar's wife would scold you?"

"Not scold, of course, but I am sure she would disapprove," said Mrs. Rose meekly.

"Ah! I thought so. Well, I will give the old lady something to talk about then. Mabin shall stay with Mrs. Dale if she wishes."

Mrs. Rose sighed heavily.

"She will wish it, of course. Girls always wish to do the very things which are not proper for them."

"You may be quite satisfied, Emily, that what I allow my daughter to do is quite proper," said Mr. Rose severely, as he left the room.

Mrs. Rose sighed. She had not told him, because it would have been of no use, that she had to be more particular than he about Mabin, because, being the girl's step-mother only, she was the more exposed to the gossip of the neighborhood—a force she dreaded—than her husband was. But she vented her ill-humor on Mabin herself, whom she informed very acidly that if she chose to go to "this Mrs. Dale," and was not comfortable with her, the fault was hers and her father's.

Mabin received these remarks meekly, rejoicing in the approaching holiday. She had nothing very serious to complain of in her treatment under her father's roof, but the snubs of her father, the tacit dislike of her step-mother, and the fact that the difference in age between her half-sisters and herself left her much alone, all combined to make her welcome the change.

Emily and Ethel, who were fourteen and twelve years of age, insipid and spiritless young persons with little brown eyes and little brown pigtails, teased her with questions about her visit of the afternoon.

"Is it true that her hair's dyed?" asked Emily, getting Mabin into a corner after tea.

"No, of course it's not," was the indignant answer.

"Oh, well, you needn't be so angry. Miss Bradley said she was sure it was, and that she knew the very stuff she used."

"Miss Bradley had better try the stuff on her own wisp then," retorted Mabin angrily.

"What is the house like inside, Mabin?" asked Ethel, who, though only twelve, was quite as great a gossip as there was in the parish.

"Why, there were chairs and tables in it, just as there are in every other house. What do you suppose it was like?"

"Mabin, don't snub the children. Their interest is very natural," said Mr. Rose peevishly from the other end of the room.

"Horsehair and mahogany, red moreen curtains, and a black marble clock on the mantelpiece," said Mabin laconically.

"Why, that doesn't sound very nice, that you should be in such a hurry to go there!" objected Ethel. "But perhaps the other rooms are better."

"Very likely," said Mabin.

But Mabin was really just a little bit alarmed at her own good fortune in getting her father's consent so easily. She had a superstitious feeling, in spite of her reputed strength of mind, that anything worth having ought to be rather difficult to get. In spite of all her loyalty to her heroine, too, she thought more often than she wished about Rudolph's ridiculous fancy that Mrs. Dale was watched. And although she always dismissed the thought by saying to herself that Rudolph was in love with the lovely widow, and therefore "fancied things," she was anxious to meet him again and to learn whether he still thought that the fair tenant of "The Towers" was being watched.

In the mean time great confusion reigned at "Stone House."

Everybody was immersed in the horrors of "packing up," and it was impossible to go upstairs without encountering people staggering under the burden of a heap of things which would have been better left behind. Even the authority of Mr. Rose, who disliked the daily routine to be disturbed, failed to get any meal eaten at the proper time, or without unnecessary hurry.

Even the fact that Mr. Rose's old friend Mrs. Haybrow was expected on a short visit before the migration, failed to check the fury of the packers. It was unfortunate that she should come at such a time, certainly. But Mrs. Rose reckoned on inflaming her friend's mind with her own zeal, and inwardly proposed orgies of competitive trunk-filling to while away the visitor's time.

Mrs. Rose secretly hoped, too, that Mrs. Haybrow, through her connections at Todcaster, would be able to furnish her husband with proofs that Mrs. Dale was not a person to be encouraged. It was not yet too late to put off Mrs. Dale, although Mr. Rose had called upon that person to thank her for the invitation to his daughter and to accept it.

It was the day of Mrs. Haybrow's expected arrival, and Mr. and Mrs. Rose had driven to the station to meet her. Mabin, wondering whether the visitor, whom she had not seen since she was a child, would be "nice," was hobbling along the garden path, rather painfully indeed, but at last without a crutch, when she heard a great rustling of the branches of the lilac bushes which grew close under the wall.

And then, above the wall, she saw the face of Rudolph.

"Oh!" cried Mabin, with a little fluttering of the heart. "I—I thought you had gone back to your ship!"

"Why, so I had," replied Rudolph, raising himself so that she had a view of his shoulders as well as of his head. "But I've come back again, you see."

"I can guess what brought you!" said Mabin, wishing the next moment that she had not uttered the words.

Rudolph took her up quickly.

"Can you? Well then, what was it?"

Mabin blushed scarlet. Of course the thought that was in her mind that the charms of the fascinating widow had drawn him to Stone. And just the least little twinge of nascent jealousy had given a sting of pique to her tone. But she would not for the world have owned to this; and the mere thought that he might have guessed it was misery. As she did not answer, Rudolph shook his head.

"I don't think you are quite as clever as you suppose," he said. "And I don't choose to tell you what brought me back. But I may just warn you that you are likely to get tired of the sight of me before I do go away altogether, as I can get as much leave as I like while my ship is at Portsmouth. Rather alarming prospect, isn't it?"

"You will get tired of being on shore, won't you?" asked Mabin, not feeling equal to answering him in his own tone, which was what her parents and the Vicarage people would have called "flippant."

"That depends," said Rudolph, looking down with interest at the dried-up blossoms of the lilac trees.

Mabin glanced at him, and began to hope nervously that she might not see too much of him. She had never seen a man whom she considered so handsome as this brown-faced young lieutenant with the merry black eyes, who made her feel so ridiculously shy and stiff. And the very attraction he had for her seemed to the simple young girl alarming, since she raised him in her maiden fancy to a pinnacle from which such a peerless creature could never descend to her.

In spite of herself her tone sounded cold and constrained, therefore, as she cut short the pause in the conversation by asking if they were all well at the Vicarage.

"Quite well, thank you," answered Rudolph demurely. "I suppose that kind inquiry is meant for a snub, isn't it? And intended to imply that I ought not to have addressed you in this informal manner over the wall,

25

but that I ought to have called in the proper manner at the other side of the house?"

"It wasn't meant to imply that," replied Mabin with solemn straightforwardness. "Only I wanted to say something, and I had nothing better to say. I must tell you that everybody says that I have no conversation."

"People allow you very few good points, according to your account."

"Quite as many as I have, though!"

"Well, at least, then you have one merit of unusual modesty."

Mabin looked up at him steadily and frankly.

"It's rather difficult for me to talk to you, because I can never tell whether you are serious or only laughing at me. Don't you rather—rather *puzzle* Mrs. Bonnington?"

"Well, I am afraid I rather—rather shock her too."

"We must all seem, down here, very antediluvian to you. There is only one person about here you can speak to in your own way."

"Mrs. Dale?"

To Mabin's fanciful and rather jealous eyes it seemed that Rudolph's color grew a little deeper as he uttered the name.

"Yes."

"Ah! You will have an opportunity of learning the art, if you are going to stay with her."

"But it is an art which will be entirely useless when I get back here again. Papa and mamma would think it rather shocking. Do you know, if they knew how lively Mrs. Dale is in her ordinary talk they wouldn't let me go to her?"

"Then I shouldn't tell them, if I were you. You will find a use for the art of conversation some day, you know, when you come across other frivolous and good-for-nothing young persons, like Mrs. Dale and me."

Mabin would rather he had not coupled his name with that of the lovely widow.

"Were Mr. and Mrs. Bonnington interested to hear you had been to see her?" asked Mabin, feeling as she spoke that this was another indiscretion.

But Rudolph began to laugh mischievously.

"They would have been extremely 'interested,' I am sure, if they had heard of it," said he. "But I have too much consideration for my parents to impart to them any information which would 'interest' them too deeply to be good for their digestions. I suppose you think that shocking, don't you?"

But Mabin was cautious. There was more than one gulf, she felt, between her and the merry young sailor, and she was not going to make them any wider.

"I'm sure you do what is best," she said modestly.

"I've got something to tell you," said he. "But it's rather a confidential communication, and these lilac bushes extend a long way. Will you come nearer to the wall? Or may I get over it?"

"You may get over if you like," said Mabin, coming as she spoke a little nearer to the bushes.

Rudolph availed himself of the permission in the twinkling of an eye, and stood beside her on the grass path under the limes, looking down at the pretty nape of the girlish neck, which showed between the soft brown hair and the plain, wide turn-down collar of pale blue linen which she wore with her fresh Holland frock.

"The man—I told you about the man I saw watching 'The Towers,' well, he has disappeared," said Rudolph, not sorry to have an excuse for whispering into such a pretty little pink ear.

"Oh! I am glad!"

"So I hope we shall see no more of him."

"And do you still think—surely you can't still think—that he was watching Mrs. Dale?"

"Oh, well, don't *know*, of course. And at any rate the slight objection I had to your going to 'The Towers' has disappeared."

Mabin felt a strange pleasure at the interest implied in this concern for her. There was a pause, broken by Mabin, who suddenly started, as if waking from a dream.

"The carriage!" cried she. "They have come back. I must go in. Good-by."

She held out her hand. He took it, and detained it a moment.

"I may come and see you sometimes, when you are at 'The Towers,' mayn't I? For old acquaintance' sake?"

"Or—for Mrs. Dale's!" said Mabin quickly, as she snatched away her hand and ran into the house.

She was not so silly as not to know where the attraction of 'The Towers' lay!

Mrs. Rose's lumbering old landau, which made such a contrast to Mrs. Dale's smart victoria, had returned from the station, and as it drove slowly along the road past 'The Towers,' Mrs. Rose was just finishing to Mrs. Haybrow a long recital of her difficulties in connection with the doubtful new resident.

Mr. Rose had chosen to come back on foot, so his wife could pour out her tale without interruption or contradiction.

"There," she cried below her breath, as they came close to the gates of 'The Towers,' "you will be able to see her. She is standing just inside the garden, calling to her little dog. Don't you think that a little dog always looks rather—rather *odd?*"

Mrs. Haybrow thought that this was somewhat severe judgment, but she did not say so. She got a good view of the mysterious lady in black; for Mrs. Dale raised her golden head as the carriage passed, and she and Mrs. Rose exchanged a rather cool bow.

To the great surprise of her companion, Mrs. Haybrow fell suddenly into a state of intense excitement.

"Why, it's Dolly Leatham, little Dolly Leatham!" she cried with evident delight. "The idea of my meeting her down here! I haven't seen the child for years."

"You know her then?" asked Mrs. Rose, in a tone which in relief was mingled with disappointment at the collapse of her own suspicions.

"I used to know her very well. She was the belle of that part of Yorkshire. The last I heard of her was that she was engaged to be married to some man who had a lot of money; and they said she was being hurried into it by her people rather against her will."

"Well, she has managed to get rid of him," said Mrs. Rose coldly. "You see she is in widow's dress now."

"Yes, so I see. Poor Dolly! It seems rather strange to find her here, so far from all her friends! And the things you have told me."

After a pause Mrs. Haybrow said decidedly: "I must call upon her to-morrow—No, I'll go and see her at once. There will be plenty of time before dinner, won't there? There's something mysterious about this, and I must find out what it is."

So, when she had had a cup of tea, Mrs. Haybrow went straight to "The Towers."

She remained there a long time, so long that Mrs. Rose wondered what the ladies could have to say to each other. And when at last Mabin, who was watching at the drawing-room window for her return, called out that she was coming up the garden, the girl added: "Oh, mamma, how pale she looks!"

"She is tired, no doubt," said Mrs. Rose, as she left the room to meet her friend as the latter came in.

But she also was surprised to see how white Mrs. Haybrow had grown.

"You should have waited until after dinner. You look quite worn out," she said. "Well, and what had your friend got to say to you?"

Mrs. Haybrow paused, as if too much exhausted to answer at once. Then she said quietly:

"I was mistaken. She was not my friend after all."

"Not your friend! Dear me! You were so long gone that we were quite sure she was."

"No. She is very nice, though, quite a charming woman."

"Ah!" exclaimed Mrs. Rose suspiciously. "But what do you think about her having Mabin?"

There was another slight pause before Mrs. Haybrow answered: "I am sure you may be quite satisfied about that."

But when dinner was over, Mrs. Haybrow got Mabin to take her to see the new ducks that Mr. Rose was so proud of; and on the way back she asked the girl whether she was very anxious for her visit to "The Towers." And finding that she was, Mrs. Haybrow added:

"And of course, dear, if anything were to happen while you were there, which seemed to you rather strange or unusual, you would write or telegraph to papa and mamma, at once, wouldn't you?"

"Of course. I see," went on Mabin, smiling, "that mamma has managed to infect you already with her own suspicions of poor Mrs. Dale."

"No, dear, she seemed to me a very nice woman indeed, and very anxious to have you. But I am getting old, and I am nervous about girls away from their homes. That is all."

And she turned the conversation to another subject.

CHAPTER V.
A STARTLING VISIT.

MRS. ROSE was not a woman of acute perceptions, but even she was vaguely conscious that there was something not quite satisfactory about the account Mrs. Haybrow had given of her visit to "The Towers."

Surely it was very strange that, after being so sure that Mrs. Dale was an old friend of hers, she should have discovered that she was mistaken! And again, if the pretty widow had really proved to be a stranger, why should Mrs. Haybrow, tired as she was after her journey, have stayed at "The Towers" so long?

And besides, Mrs. Rose could not help thinking that she had heard some name like "Dolly Leatham" before, although she had forgotten that it was from the lips of Mrs. Bonnington, and that it had been part of the backstairs gossip which Mr. Rose would have been angry with her for encouraging.

Mrs. Rose was a person in whose mind few facts long remained in a definite shape. Accustomed to have all mental processes performed for her by her husband, she lived in a state of intellectual laziness, in which her faculties had begun to rust. Mr. Rose had complete confidence in Mrs. Haybrow, who was indeed a staid, solid sort of person who inspired trust. If, therefore, Mr. Rose trusted to Mrs. Haybrow's judgment, and Mrs. Haybrow saw no objection to Mabin's visit, surely there was no need to fatigue one's self by hunting out obstacles to a very convenient arrangement.

And so it fell out that, when Mrs. Haybrow's visit was over, and the Roses started for Switzerland, Mabin saw them all off at the station, and then returned to "Stone House," to pack up the few things she had left out which she would want during her stay at "The Towers."

She had reached the portico, and was going up the steps of her home with leisurely steps, rather melancholy at the partings which had been gone through, and with a few girlish fears about her visit, when the door of the house was opened suddenly before she could ring the bell, and the parlormaid, one of the two servants who, at the request of the new tenant, had been left behind, appeared, with her finger to her lips.

Mabin stopped on the top step and looked at her with surprise.

Langton came out, and spoke in a whisper:

"Shall I pack up your things, and send them in to Mrs. Dale's to-night, Miss Mabin? Mr. Banks has come, and he seems such a queer sort of gentleman, I don't quite know how to take him yet. He came upon us quite sudden, almost as soon as the 'bus with the luggage had turned the corner, and asked sharp-like, if they were all gone. And I said 'Yes,' and he seemed relieved like, and so I didn't dare to mention you were coming back to fetch your things."

Mabin stared gloomily at Langford, who was evidently anxious to get rid of her.

"What's the matter with him? Do you think it is Mr. Banks, and not some man who's got into the house by pretending to be he?"

"Lor', Miss Mabin, I never thought of that!" cried poor Langford, turning quite white.

She had evidently entertained faint suspicions of her own, for at this suggestion she was about to fly into the house in search of the new-comer, and perhaps to brand him as an impostor, when Mabin, smiling at her alarm, caught hold of her to detain her.

"No, no, you silly girl. Of course it's all right. It's sure to be all right. He's probably eccentric, that's all. Doesn't he look the kind of person you would expect?"

"Oh, yes, Miss Mabin, he's every inch a gentleman. But—" She hesitated, apparently unable to put into appropriate words the impression the new tenant had made upon her.

"But what?"

"He is rather—rather strange-looking. I—I think he looks as if he wouldn't live long. His face has a sort of gray look, as if— Well, Miss Mabin, it's a queer thing to say, but he looks to me half-scared."

"Mad?" suggested Mabin, more with her lips and eyebrows than with her voice.

Langford nodded emphatically.

"Oh, dear!"

Then Mabin was silent, trying to recollect all that she had heard in the family circle about the gentleman who was so anxious to take the house. And she found that it did not amount to much. A rich man, a bachelor, of quiet habits, who disliked unnecessary fuss and noise, and whose references Mr. Rose's lawyer had declared to be unimpeachable—this was the sum of the family knowledge of Mr. Banks.

"Did he come quite alone?" asked Mabin, in spite of the mute entreaties of Langford that she would take herself off.

"Yes, Miss Mabin, quite alone. And he said his luggage would be sent on."

After a short pause, during which Mabin made up her mind that there was nothing to be done but to accept the new-comer as the genuine article until he proved to be an impostor, she turned reluctantly to go.

"Good-by, Langford. Bring me my things, and mind you don't forget to feed my canary. And you might come and see me sometimes in the evening, when you can get away. I think I shall be lonely."

And indeed there were tears in the eyes of the girl, who was already homesick now that she found herself thus suddenly denied admittance at the familiar portal.

It was in a very sober and chastened mood that the young girl arrived, a few minutes later, at the gate of "The Towers," but the welcome she received would have put heart into a misanthrope.

Mrs. Dale was waiting in the garden, her pretty, fair face aglow with impatience to receive her friend. She drew the arm of Mabin, who was considerably taller than herself, through hers, and led her at once into the house, to the room which Mabin had been in before.

The table was laid for luncheon, and Mabin observed with surprise that there were two places ready, although she had not promised to come till the afternoon.

"There!" cried Mrs. Dale, triumphantly, pointing to the table, "was I not inspired? The fact is," she went on, with a smile which was almost tearful, "I was so anxious for you to come that I had begun to tell myself that I should be disappointed after all, so I had your place laid to 'make believe,' like the children. And now you are really here. Oh, it seems too good to be true!"

Mabin was pleased by this reception, as she could not fail to be, but she was also a little puzzled. She was conscious of no attractions in herself which could explain such enthusiasm on her account.

"I am afraid," she said shyly, "that I shall turn out a bitter disappointment. You can't know much about girls, Mrs. Dale, or you would feel, as they all do at home, that there is a time, which I am going through now, when a girl is just as awkward and as stupid and as generally undesirable as she can possibly be."

"Hush, hush, child! You don't know anything about it. Don't you know that girls are charming, and that part of their charm lies in that very belief that they are 'all wrong,' when as a matter of fact they are everything that is right?"

"Ah! You were never gawky and awkward!"

"I wasn't tall enough to be gawky, as you like to call yourself. But five years ago, when I was eighteen, I was just as miserable as you try to make yourself, believing myself to be in everybody's way. It led to awful consequences in my case," added Mrs. Dale, the excitement going quite suddenly out of her face and voice, and giving place to a look and tone of dull despair. Mabin, who had been made to take off her hat, put her hand in that of the little widow.

"Come and see if you like your room," said Mrs. Dale, springing quickly toward the door, with a rapid change of manner. "I must tell you frankly I am afraid you won't, because this place has been constructed haphazard, without any regard to the comfort or convenience of the unfortunate people who have to live in it. Every fireplace is so placed that the chimney must smoke whichever way the wind is, and every window is specially adapted to let in the rain, when there is any, and the wind, when there isn't."

Mrs. Dale led the way as she spoke from the dining-room, and Mabin followed.

Mrs. Dale certainly exaggerated the defects of the house, but that it was inconvenient could not be denied. The side nearest to the road, where the dining-room was, had once been the whole house. It had a basement, and out of the warren of small rooms of which it had once consisted, a fairly large hall and a few fair-sized rooms had been made.

The newer but not very new portion of the house had no basement, and it was by a short flight of steps that you descended from the hall into the drawing-room, and by another short flight that you ascended to the bedroom floor. Here the same irregularity was apparent. A corridor ran through the house from end to end on this floor, broken where the new part joined the old by half a dozen steep steps.

It was to a bedroom on the higher level at the old end of the house that Mrs. Dale conducted Mabin.

"Why, it's a lovely room!" cried the girl, surprised to find herself in a big, low-ceilinged corner room lighted by three windows, and looking out, on one side, to the road, with a view of fields and sea beyond, and on the other to the garden at the back of the house, where apple-trees and gooseberry-bushes and the homely potato occupied the chief space, while the nooks were filled with the fragrant flowers of cottage gardens, with sweet-william and sweet-pea, mignonette and wallflower.

"Do you really think so? I'm so glad. I went over to Seagate the other day and got some cretonne for the curtains and the easy-chair. The old chintz there was in the room would have given you the nightmare."

Mabin had not recovered from her first impression of astonishment and admiration. The dingy dining-room, with its mahogany and horsehair, had not prepared her for this. A beautiful rug lay in front of the fireplace, which was filled with a fresh green fern.

"This will be put in the corridor outside at night," Mrs. Dale was careful to explain.

The hangings of the little brass bedstead were of cretonne with a pattern of gray-green birds and white flowers on a pale pink ground: these hangings were trimmed with lace of a deep cream tint. The rest of the furniture was enamelled white, with the exception of a dainty Japanese writing-table in one window, and a low wicker arm-chair in another.

But it was not so much in these things as in the care and taste with which all the accessories had been chosen, the silver candlesticks and tray on the dressing-table, the little Sèvres suit on the mantelpiece, that a lavish and luxurious hand was betrayed. Mabin's delighted admiration made Mrs. Dale smile, and then suddenly burst into tears.

"Don't look at me, don't trouble your head about me, child," she cried, as she turned away her head to wipe her eyes. "It was my vanity, the vanity I can't get rid of, that made me want to show you I know how to make things pretty and nice. I made the excuse to myself that it was to please you, but really I know it was to please myself!"

"But why shouldn't you please yourself and have pretty things about you?" asked Mabin in surprise. "Is there any harm in having nice things, if one has the money to buy them and the taste to choose them? I suppose it helps to keep the people that make them."

"That is what I used to say to myself, dear," said Mrs. Dale with a sigh. "But now I don't buy pretty things any more—for—for a reason." And again a look of deep pain swept across her face. But at Mabin's interested look she shook her head. "No, no," she added, in a frightened whisper, "I wouldn't tell you why for all the world!"

"But you wear pretty clothes! Or is it only that you look so pretty in them?" suggested Mabin, blushing with the fear that she was blundering again.

Mrs. Dale shook her head smiling slightly: "I have my frocks made to fit me, that's all," she said simply. "And as for these," she touched the flashing rings on her fingers, "I wear them because I'm obliged to."

Which was all sufficiently puzzling to the young girl, who, having washed her hands, was drying them on a towel so fine that this use seemed to her a sacrilege. She refrained from further remark, however, upon the luxury in which she found herself installed, and as the luncheon bell rang at that moment the two ladies went downstairs together.

But after the beautiful appointments of her room, Mabin was struck by the contrast afforded by the rest of the house, which was furnished in the usual manner, with worn carpeting in the corridor and on the stairs, and with cheap lamps on brackets and tables in the hall and passages.

At luncheon Mrs. Dale was again in high spirits. She chattered away brightly for the amusement of her young companion, who, entirely unaccustomed to so much attention, was happier than she ever remembered to have been in her life before. Mrs. Dale did not spare the eccentricities in walk and dress of the ladies in the neighborhood any more than they had spared hers.

"I don't know how you can ever be dull when such funny things come into your head!" cried simple Mabin, wiping her eyes over a hearty fit of laughing.

Mrs. Dale grew suddenly grave again.

"Ah, nothing is amusing when one is by one's self, or when one has—thoughts!" she ended in a low voice, with a different word from the one which had been in her mind. "And now let me show you my den. No, it is not a boudoir; it is nothing but a den. Come and see."

She opened a door which led from the dining-room at once into a small room, even more bare, more sombre than the other. It had evidently once served the purpose of a library or study, for there was a heavy old bookcase in one corner and a row of empty book-shelves in another. And there was the usual horsehair sofa.

By the one window, however, there was a low and comfortable, though shabby wicker chair.

"I have had this other door fastened up and the cracks filled in," said Mrs. Dale, showing a door opposite to the one by which they had entered. "It goes down by a flight of break-neck stairs into the drawing-room, a loathsome dungeon into which I never penetrate. The draught used to be strong enough to blow me away. So I thought," she went on with curious wistfulness, "I might just have that done."

Again Mabin wondered at the penitential tone; again she glanced up. But Mrs. Dale recovered herself more quickly this time, and putting the girl gently into the wicker chair, while she curled herself up on the horsehair sofa, she drew Mabin out and encouraged the girl by sympathetic questions, and by still more sympathetic listening, to lay bare some of the recesses of her young heart.

The afternoon passed quickly; and when Mrs. Dale, springing suddenly off the sofa after a silence, ran away into the dining-room to ask about certain dainties which she had ordered from town for Mabin's benefit, but which had failed to arrive that morning, the girl was left in a state of happy excitement, thinking what a picture the little golden-haired creature had made as she sat curled up on the sofa, and wondering how she could have been so ungrateful as to imagine she could be anything but happy under the same roof with Mrs. Dale.

Mabin looked idly out of the window, and craned her neck to see if she could catch a glimpse of the sea. But this was the north side of the house, and the sea was on the southwest; so she failed. But as she looked out, she saw a fly drive slowly up the road, and was surprised to find that the solitary occupant, an elderly lady with gray hair, and a hard, forbidding face, stared at her fixedly through a pair of gold eyeglasses as if she felt some personal interest in her. Mabin felt herself blush, for she was sure she had never seen the lady before.

Just as she drew her head in she heard the cab stop at the front gate. Mrs. Dale's voice, talking brightly to the parlormaid, came to Mabin's ears through the door, which had been left ajar. Then she heard a knock at the front door, and the parlormaid went to answer it.

"Mabin, come here," cried Mrs. Dale from the next room. "I want to show you——"

The words died on her lips; and Mabin, who was in the act of coming into the dining-room in obedience to her call, stopped short, and, after a moment's consideration of what she ought to do, retreated into the smaller room and shut the door behind her.

But she had been in time to witness a strange meeting. For the elderly lady whom she had seen in the cab had appeared at the outer door of the dining-room as she had shown herself at the inner one, and it was at the sight of her that Mrs. Dale had stopped short in her speech, with a look of abhorrence and terror on her face.

The elder lady spoke at once, in a harsh, commanding voice. She was very tall, erect, and stately, handsomely dressed in black, altogether a commanding personality. Her voice rang through the room, and reached Mabin's ears, striking the girl with terror too.

"I am afraid I have taken you by surprise."

"I suppose," answered Mrs. Dale in a low voice, "that was what you intended to do."

"I am sorry to see you meet me in that spirit. I have come with every wish for your good. I think it is not right that you should be left here by yourself, as you hold no intercourse, of course, with the people of the neighborhood."

There was a pause, which Mrs. Dale would not break.

"I propose, therefore," went on the elder lady, "to stay with you myself, at least for a little while."

Mrs. Dale, who had remained standing, as her visitor did also, turned upon her quickly:

"That I will not put up with."

"That is scarcely courteous, surely?"

"There is no question of lip-courtesy between you and me. You, and no one else, have been the cause of all that has happened, and I refuse, absolutely refuse, to stay under the same roof with you for a single day."

In the mean time poor Mabin, frightened and uncertain what to do, had in the first place put her hands to her ears so that she might not play the part of unwilling eavesdropper. But as the voices grew too loud for her to avoid hearing what the ladies said, she made a frantic rush for the door, and presented herself, breathless, blushing, in the doorway.

"Oh, I—I can't help hearing what you say!" cried she, glancing from the forbidding face of the visitor to Mrs. Dale, who looked prettier than ever in her anger.

"My dear, it doesn't matter," said Dorothy gently.

But the elder lady broke in:

"It does matter very much. This is not a fit house for a young girl while you live in it."

And turning to Mabin, she said with a sudden burst of vindictive feeling: "Go home at once to your proper guardians. The woman you are now with is a——"

Before she could utter the word which was ready to her lips, Mrs. Dale interrupted her. Springing between the other two women with a low cry, she addressed the elder lady with such a torrent of passion that both Mabin and the visitor could only listen without an attempt to stop her.

"You shall not say it! You shall not tell her?! You know that she was safe with me, as if she had been in her own home. You have spoilt her happiness with me, because you knew it made me happy. But you shall not contaminate her with your wicked words. Go, child." She seized Mabin by the arm, and ran with her to the outer door of the dining-room. "Run away. I will find you when this woman is gone."

And the next moment Mabin found herself in the hall, with the dining-room door closed.

CHAPTER VI.

MR. BANKS.

THERE was silence in the room for a few minutes after the abrupt dismissal of Mabin. Mrs. Dale made a perfunctory gesture of invitation to her unwelcome visitor to be seated, and threw herself into a hard horsehair-covered armchair by the window, which she carefully closed.

The visitor, however, remained standing. She was evidently rather astonished at the high-handed behavior of the culprit whom she had come to examine, and uncertain how to deal with her. At last she said in a very cutting tone:

"I suppose I ought not by this time to be surprised at your behaving in an unbecoming manner to me, or to anybody. But as you pretended to profess some penitence for your awful sin on the last occasion of our meeting, I own I was carried away by my indignation when I found you receiving visitors, and young girl visitors. Surely you must recognize how improper such conduct is?"

"And which do you suppose is the more likely to do her harm? To stay with me knowing nothing, or to hear from your lips the awful thing you were going to tell her? Why, the poor child would never have got over the shock!"

"It would have been less harmful to her soul than constant communication with you, impenitent as you are!"

"You have no right to say that to me. How can you see into my heart?"

"I judge you by your actions. I find you here, talking and laughing, and enjoying yourself. And I hear that you have already created a most unfavorable impression in the neighborhood by your rudeness to people who have wished to be civil to you."

"Was it not your own wish that I should shut myself up?"

"Yes, but in an humble, not in a defiant, manner. And then you drive about as if nothing had happened, and excite remarks by your appearance alone, which is not the appearance of a disconsolate widow."

"By whose wish was it that I bought a carriage?"

"By mine, I suppose," replied the other frigidly, "but I meant a brougham, so that you could go about quietly, not an open and fashionable one, for you to show yourself off!"

"Well, I refuse to drive about in a stuffy, shut-up carriage. I am quite ready to walk, if you wish me to put the carriage down. And I can quite well do with less money than what you allow me. But I maintain the right to spend my allowance, whatever it may be, exactly as I please. Because one has committed one fault——"

"Fault!" almost shrieked the visitor. "One grave and deadly sin."

"Because I have done wrong, great wrong," replied Mrs. Dale. And even to this antagonistic woman her voice shook on the words, "You have no right to think that I am never to lead an independent life. You have no right to the control of my actions. All that you can demand is that I should live decently and quietly. As long as I do so I ought to be, I *will* be, as free as ever."

"But," persisted the other, "you seem not to understand what decency requires. In the first place it is imperatively necessary," and as she said this there was a look of genuine anxiety in her eyes, "that you should hold no intercourse whatever with persons of the opposite sex."

Mrs. Dale said nothing to this; and the look of questioning solicitude in the face of the other grew deeper.

"Surely," she asked at last, "you must see this yourself?"

"That," answered Mrs. Dale deliberately, "is also a matter which rests entirely with me. I won't be dictated to on that subject any more than on any other."

"Well, then, I warn you that I shall have to keep you in strict surveillance, and that if I hear of your encouraging, or even permitting, the attentions of any man, young or old, I shall feel myself bound in honor to put him in possession of the facts of your history."

"And if you do," retorted Mrs. Dale, rising and speaking in a low tone full of fire and passionate resentment, "if you interfere with me in my quiet and harmless life by telling any person whom I choose to call my friend the horrible thing that you hold over my head, I will break away from you and your surveillance once and for all. I will have the whole story published in the papers, with your share in it as well as mine, and let the world decide which of us is the most to blame: the young woman who has wrecked and poisoned her whole life by one rash and wicked act, or the old one who drove her to it, and then used it forever afterward to goad and madden her!"

She paused, and leaned against the table, white to the lips with intense excitement, panting with her own emotion. The other lady had grown white too, and she looked frightened as she answered:

"You are allowing your passion to carry you away again. I should have thought you had been cured of that." The younger lady shuddered, but said nothing; "I was bound to put you on your guard, that was all."

Mrs. Dale moved restlessly. Her face was livid and moist, her hands were shaking:

"Surely you have done that!" she said ironically. "Even the Inquisitors of Spain used to let their victims have a little rest from the torture sometimes; just to let the creatures get up their strength again, to give more sport on a future occasion!"

The visitor affected to be offended by this speech, and drew herself up in a dignified manner. But it was possible to imagine that she felt just a little shame, or a little twinge of remorse, for her persistent cruelty, for she went so far as to offer a cold hand to Mrs. Dale as she prepared to go.

Mrs. Dale looked as if she would have liked to refuse the hand, but did not dare. She touched the black glove with white, reluctant fingers, and let it go at once.

"Good-by, Dorothy," said the elder lady "I am sure you will believe, when you come to yourself and think it over, that I have only your interests at heart in the advice I have given you. No, you need not come to the door. I shall take just one walk round to look at your garden before I go. I have a cab waiting."

She sailed out of the room, the jet fringes on her gown and mantle making a noise which set Mrs. Dale's teeth on edge.

As soon as she was alone, Dorothy threw herself face downward on the hard sofa and burst into a passion of tears and sobs, which rendered her deaf and blind and unconscious of everything but the awful weight at her heart, which she must carry with her to her grave, and of the cruelty which had revived in its first intensity the old, weary pain.

She was mad, desperate with grief. She felt that it was more than she could bear; that the remorse gnawing at her heart, the more bitterly for the pleasure of the morning, had reached a point where it became intolerable, where the strength of a woman must give way.

And then when she had crawled out of the room, with smarting eyes and aching head, and found the way up to her own shabby, gloomy room with staggering feet, there came to her ear from the garden the sound of a fresh, girlish voice, uttering words which were balm to the wounded soul.

"I don't care," Mabin was saying to some unseen person among the yew trees on the lawn, "I don't care what she's done. She is a sweet woman, and I love her all the more for having to be preached to by that old cat!"

No eloquence, no smoothly rounded periods of the most brilliant speaker in the universe could have conveyed to poor unhappy Dorothy half the solace of those inelegant words! She began to smile, all red-eyed as she was, and to feel that there was something worth living for in the world after all. And when she had bathed her face, and lain down for a little ease to her aching head, she was able presently to look out with an impulse of pleasure at the bright green of the lawn, where the shadows of the tall elms were growing long, and to listen to the sound of young voices talking and laughing, and to feel that there was something left in life after all.

The voices, as she knew, were those of Mabin and Rudolph. The Vicar's son had called, with a huge bunch of flowering rushes, for Mrs. Dale, while the mysterious visitor was with her. The parlormaid, therefore, had informed him that Mrs. Dale was engaged, but that Miss Rose was in the garden; and he had lost no time in going in search of the latter.

He was surprised to find her in a state of great distress, shedding furtive tears, and trying to hide a face eloquent of grief.

"May I ask what's the matter?" he asked, when she had begun to talk about the flowers and the trees, in a rather broken and unmanageable voice.

"Oh, I don't know whether I ought to tell you!"

"Well, look here. I'll go as far as the wall that shuts in the kitchen-garden; that's on the other side of the house, you know. I'll walk very slowly, and if I find any caterpillars on the gooseberries I'll pick them off. That will give you a long time. And when I come back I shall expect you to have made up your mind whether you can tell me or not. Only," added he wistfully, "I do hope you will make up your mind that you can; for I'm 'dying of curiosity,' as the ladies say."

"No, they don't say that," said Mabin cantankerously. "Women are much less curious than the men, really. I wouldn't have heard what I did for worlds if I could have helped it. And you are 'dying' to know it!"

"Well, I won't argue with you," replied Rudolph philosophically, as he walked slowly, according to his promise, in the direction of the kitchen-garden.

Mabin watched him, drying her eyes, and asking herself whether there would be any harm in confiding in him. She felt the want of some one of whom she could take counsel in this extremely embarrassing situation for a young girl to find herself in. If only Mrs. Haybrow had been at hand! She was a motherly woman, whose sympathy could be as much relied upon as her advice. Not once did it occur to the girl to write to her step-mother, who would have consulted Mr. Rose, with results disastrous to the reputation of poor little Mrs. Dale. For it was not to be supposed that a father could allow his daughter to remain in the house of a lady about whom there was certainly more than a suspicion of irregularity of some sort.

She was pondering these things, in a helpless and bewildered fashion, anxious to do right, and not quite certain where the right lay, when she heard a firm step on the gravel path, and, looking round, saw that the austere-looking lady who had descended so abruptly upon Mrs. Dale was coming toward her.

Mabin would have liked to run away, and did indeed give one glance and make one step, in the direction of the little path between the yews which led round to the kitchen garden.

But the person she had to deal with was not to be put off in that manner.

"Stop!" she cried, in such an imperious voice that Mabin obeyed at once. "I want to speak to you."

Mabin glanced up at the hard, cold face, and her heart rose in rebellion at the thought that the severe expression was for poor Mrs. Dale. She drew up her head with a flash of spirit, and waited quietly for what the elder lady had to say.

"What is your name? And where do you live?" asked the lady.

At first, guessing that this vixenish woman wanted to communicate with her friends about the desirability of removing her from "The Towers," Mabin felt inclined to refuse to answer. But a moment's reflection showed her that it would be easy for the lady to get the information she wanted from the servants; so she said:

"My name is Mabin Rose, and my father is on his way to Geneva."

"And how did he become acquainted with——" she paused, and added in a peculiar tone, as if the name stuck in her throat—"with Mrs. Dale?"

"They were neighbors," answered Mabin shortly.

"You had better write to him and ask him to take you away," said the lady. "There are circumstances——"

But Mabin put her hands up to her ears.

"Not a word!" cried she. "I won't hear a word. I beg your pardon for having to be so rude, but I won't listen to you; I won't hear a word against my friend."

She was prepared in her excitement for some sort of struggle. But the lady merely glared at her through her long-handled eye-glasses in disgust, and with a pinched smile and a contemptuous movement of the shoulders, walked majestically back toward the house.

The parlormaid, trying to look discreetly incurious, was standing by the gate, to open it for the visitor to go out. But the lady paused to enter into conversation with her; and Mabin was filled with indignation, believing, as she did, that the stranger's motives were not above suspicion. And she caught the words which the maid uttered just before the cab drove away with the stranger:

"Very well, my lady."

And then she heard Rudolph's voice behind her.

"Well, have you had time to make up your mind?"

She started and turned quickly. He was surprised to see that all traces of tears had disappeared, and that her face was burning with excitement.

"Oh, yes, yes. I must tell you now! If I didn't, I should have to go and confide in Mrs. Dale's little dog!"

"Well, I promise to be quite as discreet."

"That cab that you saw drive away had in it a woman who came here to see Mrs. Dale, and who told me that I ought to go away and not stay in the same house with her!"

"Well?"

"Well! Is that all you have to say? Aren't you disgusted? You who pretend to like and admire Mrs. Dale so much?"

"There is no pretense in it. I do like and admire her very much. But how can you be astonished after the warnings you have had?"

Mabin looked at him with wide open eyes.

"I thought," she said rather coldly, "that you would take her part."

"Yes, so I will; so I do. But I don't feel quite sure whether you ought to."

"And why not? Why, since I like and pity her too, shouldn't I take her part too?"

For a few minutes Rudolph was silent.

"You're a girl," said he at last.

"But that's no reason why I should act meanly!"

"Ah, well, if it's not a reason, it's an excuse."

"I don't think so. I like to stand by my friends. I haven't many; I haven't any I like better than Mrs. Dale. So, whatever it is that she has done, I shall stay with her as long as she wants me, and do all I can to prevent these stories getting to papa's and mamma's ears."

Rudolph looked at her fair face, which was aglow with generous enthusiasm, and smiled in hearty approval.

"That's right," said he warmly. "And if people are too much shocked by your daring, why you can marry me, you know, and when once you're married you can snap your fingers at them all."

But at this suggestion Mabin had suddenly turned pale. In truth she liked Rudolph well enough not to be able to bear a jest on the idea of marriage with him. Naturally he was surprised and even a little hurt by the abrupt change in her sensitive face.

"Oh, you need not look so frightened," said he, laughing. "I only suggested it as a last resource in case of extremity."

"Oh, I know. But—what extremity?"

"If people think the worse of you for standing by your friend."

Mabin drew her tall, slim figure to its fullest height.

"I shouldn't care," said she. "I should snap my fingers at them in any case."

Rudolph considered her for a few silent minutes. It was then that she uttered the words which reached Mrs. Dale's ears, and startled while they comforted the unhappy woman:

"I don't care—I don't care what she's done. She is a sweet woman, and I love her all the more for having to be preached to by that old cat."

And then she noticed that she and her companion were standing rather near an open window, and she walked quickly back to the lawn and the elm trees.

"What old cat?"

"Didn't you see her? A tall woman with a face carved in marble. She was driving away as you came back."

"I didn't see much of her. Do you know who she is?"

"No. She's a 'ladyship,' from what the maid said. And she looks like one, which ladyships hardly ever do. That's all I know."

"A relation of Mrs. Dale's, I suppose?"

"Ye-e-s, I suppose so, from the things she said. But oh! Mrs. Dale has never done anything to deserve such a relation as that!"

"Poor thing! No. But one can't help feeling curious."

"I can help it," cried Mabin stoutly. "I know how these spiteful old women make mountains out of molehills, and I will never believe that it isn't a molehill in this case after all."

Rudolph looked at her curiously.

"Do you know who it is that has taken your father's house?" he asked in a dry tone.

"Yes, a Mr. Banks. He came this morning, as soon as papa and mamma were out of the house."

"And do you know anything about him? Is he a friend of your father's?"

"No. He was looking for a furnished house down here, and heard that we wanted to let ours. It was all arranged through his solicitor and papa's. He is an invalid, I believe, come here for change of air. Why do you ask?"

"Because I was in the lane between your garden and this just before I came here, and I saw a man walking along the grass path, and recognized him as the man I found watching Mrs. Dale a fortnight ago. There's a secret for you, in return for yours."

Mabin looked frightened. She remembered her own suspicions that the man who had presented himself as Mr. Banks was an impostor.

"What was he like?" she asked.

"He was very thin and pale, and he looked like a gentleman. I could hardly tell whether he was old or young."

"Perhaps," she faltered, "he isn't Mr. Banks at all!"

Rudolph did not answer immediately. Then he said slowly:

"I wonder what he has come for?"

Mabin stared at him stupidly. As they stood silent in the quiet garden, they both heard a slight rustling of the leaves, a cracking of the branches, near the wall which divided the garden from the lane.

CHAPTER VII.
A STRANGE FANCY.

"WHAT was that?" asked Mabin with a shiver.

She and Rudolph had both turned instinctively toward the spot from which the rustling noise had come.

"A cat, most likely," answered Rudolph.

But Mabin shook her head.

"I saw something," whispered she. "It was not a cat, it was not an animal at all; it was a man."

Perhaps Rudolph had his suspicions, for he expressed no surprise. Before he could answer her they heard the crackling and rustling again, but at a little distance. The intruder was making his way through the shrubbery.

"Won't you find out who it is?" whispered the girl again.

Rudolph hesitated.

"Perhaps I know," said he shortly. "But if you wish, of course I can make sure."

Then, with evident reluctance, and taking no pains to go noiselessly, he followed the intruder through the bushes, and was in time to catch a glimpse of him as he disappeared over a part of the fence that was in a broken-down condition. Rudolph did not attempt to continue his pursuit, but contented himself with waiting until he heard the side gate in the garden wall of "Stone House" swing back into its place with a loud creaking noise. Then he went back to Mabin. She was standing where he had left her, on the broad gravel path under the faded laburnum. The shadows were very deep under the trees by this time, and in the half-light her young face, with its small, delicate features, its dreamy, thoughtful eyes, full of the wonder at the world of the very young, looked so pretty that for the moment Rudolph forgot the errand on which he had been sent, and approached her with no thought of anything but the beauty and the sweetness of her face.

She, all unconscious of this, woke him into recollection with one abrupt word: "Well?"

"Oh!" almost stammered he, "it was as I thought, the same person that I saw watching before."

"And he went into our garden. I heard the gate," said Mabin with excitement. "It must be this Mr. Banks. Oh, who do you think he is? What do you think he has come for?"

Rudolph was silent. Even to the least curious mind the circumstances surrounding both him and Mrs. Dale could not seem other than mysterious. If he were a detective, and he certainly did not look like one, surely he would not go to work in this extravagant manner, by renting a large and expensive house merely for the purpose of watching his next-door neighbor. Neither, it might be supposed, would he set to work in such a clumsy fashion as to be caught making his investigations at the very outset. Rudolph felt that the whole affair was a mystery to which he could not pretend to have the shadow of a clew. He confessed this to Mabin.

"I wish," he went on, in a gentle tone, "that I had known something of this before your father went away."

"Why?" asked Mabin in surprise, and with something like revolt in her tone.

"Because I should have told him something, just enough at any rate to have made him take you away with him."

Mabin was for a moment dumb with surprise.

"What," she stammered at last, "after all your talk about my being right to stand by my friend?"

"Even after all that," assented Rudolph with decision. "The matter is getting too serious," he went on gravely. "I am afraid myself of what may be going to happen."

"Then," retorted the girl, "for all your talk about meanness being excusable in a girl, I can be a better friend than you."

Rudolph smiled.

"Ah," said he, "you forget that with you it is only a question of your friendship for Mrs. Dale. Now I have to think of both of you."

"You need not trouble yourself about me, I assure you."

"But that is just what I must do, madam, even at the risk of your eternal displeasure," said Rudolph, with a mock-heroic air which concealed real anxiety. "You are not only daring enough, you are too daring where your heart is concerned, and it is the business of your friends to see that you do not suffer for your generosity." He spoke with so much quiet decision that Mabin was impressed and rather frightened, and it was with a sudden drop from haughtiness to meekness that she then asked:

"What are you going to do, then?"

Rudolph hesitated.

"What I should like to do," said he, "is to take you to my mother's——"

Mabin almost screamed.

"You won't do that," she said quietly, with her lips very tightly closed.

"She would be very kind to you," suggested Rudolph gently, pleadingly.

He knew the prospect was not an enticing one, but he was not so quick as the girl to see all its disadvantages.

"And don't you see that it would set them all saying the most dreadful things about poor Mrs. Dale, if I were to leave her suddenly like that? I shouldn't think of such a thing. It would be cruel as well as cowardly. She would never be able to stay in Stone after that."

"I don't think she will be able to stay in any case," said Rudolph gloomily. "If she is persecuted by this spy on the one hand, and by the old woman on the other, it isn't likely that she will be able to stay here long."

A new idea flashed suddenly into Mabin's mind and then quickly found expression:

"Do you suppose," she asked, "that this man, this Mr. Banks, is paid by the old lady to spy upon Mrs. Dale? The old lady must be very rich, I think, and she is eccentric evidently."

But Rudolph was inclined to think this idea far-fetched. From what he had seen of the mysterious spy he had come to quite another conclusion, one that at present he did not care to communicate to Mabin, for fear of alarming her unnecessarily.

"Of course it is possible that the man may be a paid detective," admitted he doubtfully, "but there was nothing of the cut of the ex-detective about your Mr. Banks. And now," went on Rudolph, who found Mabin herself a more interesting mystery than the unknown man, "let us forget all about him for a little while, and go up to the old seat where the trees leave off, before it gets too dark for us to see the sea. You remember the old seat, and how we used to trespass to get at it, don't you?"

Mabin blushed a little. She remembered the old seat very well; an old broken-down bench supported on the stumps of a couple of felled trees, just on the edge of the plantation belonging to "The Towers." Being conveniently near both to "Stone House" and the Vicarage, the children of both houses had established, in those far-off years which Rudolph was recalling, a right to tread down the old fence at that particular point, and to hold wonderful picnics of butterscotch and sour apples.

"We won't go up there now," she said, with a sudden demureness which contrasted strongly with the eagerness she had shown while discussing the persecution of Mrs. Dale. "It's getting dark, and rather cold, I think, and besides, I hope by this time that Mrs. Dale may be ready to see us again."

Rudolph felt snubbed. The girl's manner was so precise, so stiff, that it was impossible for him to understand that her sudden primness was only a relapse into her ferocious girlish modesty. He followed her without a word toward the house, and there just inside the portico they saw the slight figure in black looking like a pathetic vision in the gloaming, with its white, tear-stained face and slender little jewelled hands.

"Well?" said Mrs. Dale. And her voice was hoarse and broken. "I have been waiting here for you, wondering where you had gone. I had almost begun to think," she went on, with assumed playfulness, which did not hide the fact that her fear had been real, "that you had run away from me altogether."

Mabin lost her awkwardness, her stiffness, her shy, girlish reserve in an instant; moved by strong pity and affection, she took the two steps which brought her under the portico, and stooping, flung her arms round the little figure.

"You didn't—really?" she whispered hoarsely. "Oh, I hope not, I hope not!"

Mrs. Dale could not answer. But Mabin felt her frame quiver from head to foot, and heard the sound of a stifled sob. Rudolph stepped noiselessly out into the garden again.

"My dear, my dear child," murmured Mrs. Dale, when she had recovered some of her self-possession by a strong effort, "you would have been quite justified if you had gone. But I am glad, oh, so glad, that you have waited for me to drive you away."

"You won't do that!" cried Mabin, starting back, and seeing with surprise in the fair, blue-eyed face an expression of strong resolution. "After pretending you were so glad to have me!"

"It was no pretence, believe me!" said Mrs. Dale with a sad little smile. "But I have got to send you away all the same. It would not be right to keep you here, now that I see the persecution I am to be subjected to still." And her blue eyes flashed angrily as she spoke. But the next moment her face changed again, and she added quickly, "I have deserved it all. More than all. I am not complaining of that; I have no right to complain. Only—she might have spared you. I should have done you no harm; you would have learnt no evil from me, wicked as I am."

The girl interrupted her, with a frightened face, and speaking in an eager whisper:

"Oh, hush, hush! You are not wicked. It is dreadful to hear you say such things! I will not let you say them. You have the kindest heart in the world; if you have ever done wrong, you are sorry, bitterly sorry. Wicked people are never sorry. Let me stay with you and comfort you if I can, by showing you how happy it makes me to be with you!"

Mrs. Dale shook her head. She did not, however, repeat in words her resolve that Mabin must go, though the girl guessed by the expression of her face that her mind was made up on the subject.

They stood silently looking out at the soft beauties of the twilight, the greens as they melted into grays blending in such a tender harmony of color that the sight seemed to supply a balm, through tear-dimmed eyes, to their heavy hearts; the scent of the roses came to them across the broad space of gravel, too, mingled with the pleasantly acrid perfume of the limes.

Rudolph's step, as he took advantage of the silence to thrust himself again upon the notice of the ladies, startled them both.

"Now you've spoilt it all!" cried Mrs. Dale, in a tone which was meant to be one of light-hearted pleasantry, but which betrayed too plainly the difficulty she had in assuming it. "The garden looked like a fairy picture till you rushed in and ruined the perspective. Aren't you going to apologize?"

"No. The picture wanted human interest, so I painted myself into the canvas, just to satisfy your artistic susceptibilities. I am sorry to find you so ungrateful. I hope you, Mabin, have more appreciation?"

But the girl's eyes were full of tears, and not being used to this light strain of talk, she could not answer, except by a few mumbled words which had neither sense nor coherence. Mrs. Dale put up her hand—she had to stretch it up a long way—and smoothed the girl's pretty brown hair.

"Don't tease her," she said softly. "Mr. Bonnington, I mustn't ask you to dine with us, but I would if I might."

"And why mustn't you?" asked Rudolph.

"Well, because, in the miserably equivocal position I am in, it would be a pleasure—if I may take it for granted that it would be a pleasure to you, as it would certainly be to me—dearly bought. The Vicar would strongly disapprove; your mother would be shocked beyond measure."

"But I shouldn't mind that, I assure you. I've shocked my mother and excited the disapproval of my father so often that they don't expect anything else from me. Besides, I am afraid you flatter yourself too much in believing that you have such an enviable peculiarity; if you were to issue invitations to the whole parish to a garden party, or a dinner, or anything you liked, I'm afraid you would be disappointed to find that everybody would come."

"Perhaps they would think there was safety in numbers, and that, fortified by the presence of everybody else, they could gaze at the monster in security!" suggested Mrs. Dale with a smile.

"In the mean time how much nearer have I got to get to inviting myself to dinner this evening?" said Rudolph, with a subdued voice and a meek manner.

"Ah, well, for Mabin's sake then, I spare you the humiliation and invite you myself. You shall stay to amuse her, since I am afraid she would find me a very dreary companion."

"Indeed I shouldn't," cried Mabin, blushing deeply, and speaking with as much energy as if the presence of Rudolph were an injury. "I should like nothing better than an evening alone with you."

Rudolph drew a deep sigh, and even Mrs. Dale could not suppress a smile at the girl's unconscious *gaucherie*. When Mabin realized what a stupid thing she had said, she was of course too much ashamed of herself to laugh at her clumsy words, and fell, instead, into a stiff silence which the others found it impossible to make her break except by demure monosyllabic answers.

When they went into the dining-room, therefore, the evening did not promise to be a lively one. Mrs. Dale seemed to find it impossible to shake off the effects of the visit of her persecutor. Rudolph was oppressed by fears for both the ladies, and by doubts whether his presence there was not an indiscretion which would make matters worse for both of them. While Mabin, perplexed and troubled by a score of unaccustomed sensations, was the most silent, the most distressed of all.

Daylight was still streaming in from the West as they took their seats at the table in the dingily furnished room. Mrs. Dale gave a little shudder as she glanced from the "furnished house" knives to the commonplace dinner service.

"Ah!" she said, "it is not like this that I used to entertain my friends. My little dinners had quite a reputation—once!"

Then, as if she felt that these regrets were worse than vain, she turned the subject abruptly, while a spasm of pain for the moment convulsed her face.

Rudolph on his side was sorry she had mentioned the "little dinners." They suggested a past life in which there had been something more than frivolity; something with which he would have dissociated Mrs. Dale if he could. But innocent Mabin, wishing to say something, brought the conversation back to the point it had left.

"But why can't you have pretty dinners now, if you like to?"

Mrs. Dale's fair face grew whiter as she answered gently:

"I will tell you—presently—some day—why I don't have anything pretty or nice about me now."

And Mabin, feeling that she had touched a painful chord, became more silent than ever.

Perhaps it was her sudden subsidence into absolute gloom which caused the other two to make a great effort to restore something like animation to the talk. And being both young, and of naturally high spirits, they succeeded so well that before the meal which had begun so solemnly was over, Mrs. Dale and Rudolph were talking and laughing as if there had never been a shadow upon either of their lives. At first they made brave attempts to drag Mabin into the conversation. But as these efforts were in vain, it naturally ended in her being left out of the gayety, and in her sitting entrenched in a gloomy silence of her own.

And when dinner was over, and they all went into the little adjoining room which Mrs. Dale called her "den," it was quite natural that Mrs. Dale should sit down at the piano, in the good-natured wish to leave the young people to entertain each other; and equally natural that Rudolph, on finding that Mabin had nothing to say to him, and that she was particularly frigid in her manner, should go over to the piano, and by coaxing Mrs. Dale to sing him his favorite songs and then hers, should continue the brisk flirtation begun at the dinner-table.

Mabin had brought it all upon herself, and she tried to persuade herself that it was quite right and natural, and that she did not mind. And when Rudolph was gone, and she was alone with her hostess, she succeeded in persuading her that she had not felt neglected, but had enjoyed the merriment she had refused to share.

But when she got upstairs into her pretty bedroom, after bidding Mrs. Dale good-night, she had the greatest difficulty in keeping back the tears which were dangerously near her proud eyes.

She did not care for Rudolph, of course not; she wanted him to fall in love with Mrs. Dale, if indeed he had not already done so, and marry her and console her for all her troubles, and stop the persecution of "the cat." But somehow this hope, this wish, did not give her all the unselfish satisfaction it ought to have done.

And Mabin, wondering what had happened to take the prettiness out of the room and the pleasure out of her acquaintance with Mrs. Dale, fell asleep with her heart heavy and full of nameless grief.

She woke with a start to find a white figure standing motionless in the middle of the room. Mabin sprang up in bed and rubbed her eyes. Was she awake? Or was she only dreaming that the body of a dead woman, stiff, rigid, but in an upright position, was standing like a marble statue between the bed and the nearest window?

She leaped out of bed, and, not without uncanny fears, touched the statuesque figure.

"Mrs. Dale!" she almost shrieked, as the great eyes suddenly turned and fixed a blank, wild gaze upon her face. "Oh, what has happened? What is the matter?"

The figure, which, in white night garments, had looked so unlike the black-robed widow that she had not recognized it, trembled from head to foot. The lips parted, but at first no word escaped them. At last with a strong effort she uttered these words:

"Let me stay here. Let me sit in this arm-chair till morning. Oh, I will not hurt you, or frighten you. But if I go back I shall go mad! This house is haunted, haunted! I have seen——"

A hoarse rattle in her throat seized her, threatened to choke her. With one wild glance round, peering into the corners of the room, she flung herself on the floor, and buried her face in the chair.

CHAPTER VIII.
A HAUNTED HOUSE.

MABIN was taken so thoroughly by surprise, on seeing the wild self-abandonment of her unhappy companion, that for a few minutes she stood staring at the crouching figure on the floor like one only half-awake.

Was this really Mrs. Dale, this haggard, panting creature with the hoarse voice, the twitching hands, the wide eyes full of unspeakable terror. Mabin's sympathy was ready, but at first she did not dare to offer it. Such terrible anguish, such paralyzing fear, as that from which the miserable woman was suffering, was something surely beyond her poor powers of comfort! And even as the girl advanced timidly a step nearer to her grief-stricken friend, there flashed into her mind the horrible question: What must this secret be which was locked in the widow's breast, that could throw her into such paroxysms of abject terror? For, not unnaturally, Mabin came to the conclusion that the vision which had alarmed Mrs. Dale was one of the results of the remorse from which she owned that she was suffering.

"Don't! Don't sob like that! You will make yourself ill; you will indeed. There is nothing, there is nobody here to frighten you," said the girl at last, drawing a little closer to the crouching figure, but not yet daring to touch her, or to speak in a tone louder than a whisper.

At the first sound of her voice, Mrs. Dale had started, and raised her head quickly, turning to the girl's view a face so much altered, so drawn, so old-looking, that she hardly recognized the features of the lovely widow. Then, when the voice ceased, she glanced round the room again, with the same hunted, anxious look as before.

"Nothing—nobody to frighten me!" she repeated in a shaking voice. "No, of course not, of course not. How silly I have been! I am afraid I frightened you, dear,—with my dreams, my silly fancies!"

She struggled, as if worn out and exhausted by her emotion, to gain her feet. Timidly, gently, Mabin helped her to rise.

"I'm very glad I was here," answered Mabin, in kindly tones that sent a shiver of grateful recognition through her agitated companion. "Do you feel better now?"

"Yes, oh, yes, I am all right. I am not ill. I am so much ashamed of myself for disturbing you. I don't know how to apologize," answered Mrs. Dale, trying bravely to speak in her usual tone, but glancing at the door and then back to the windows as she uttered the words: "It must have been a dream, of course, that frightened me."

And then, quite suddenly, she broke down again, and slipping from the supporting arm of her young companion, she threw herself into the wicker arm-chair, and burst into a passion of tears. Uncertain what to do, Mabin, in her sympathy and kindness, did exactly the right thing. She drew another chair besides the wicker one, sat down in it, and putting her right arm round Mrs. Dale's shoulder, and holding the poor lady's trembling fingers in her own, remained in perfect silence until the first ebullition of violent grief had passed away.

"I shall never forget your kindness, child, never," said Mrs. Dale, when, as suddenly as it had begun, her passion of tears ended. "You have saved me from going mad—yes, mad. I—I must leave you now, or you won't get any rest."

She rose as she spoke; but Mabin saw that the panic of terror which had been upon her at her entrance was regaining its hold upon her as she approached the door. With her fingers on the handle she stopped, and seemed once more to grow rigid with fear.

Mabin was by her side in an instant.

"Stay here," she said. "You will have the dream again perhaps, if you go away by yourself."

At these words a shiver ran through Mrs. Dale, and she faltered.

"It must have been that gloomy room!" she said at last in a whisper. "And the effect of her visit! But it will kill me if it comes again!" Suddenly she turned to Mabin. "May I lie on the sofa until the morning?" she asked piteously. "I won't disturb you. I feel as if I should be safe from—it—in here with you?"

The wistful pleading in her eyes brought the tears to Mabin's.

"Of course you must stay," she cried heartily. "And I do hope you will get to sleep, and not have any more dreams."

Very quietly Mrs. Dale lay down on the couch between the windows, and drawing the sofa blanket over her, and refusing any other covering, she closed her eyes. Mabin knew that this apparent tranquillity was assumed only, and she placed herself on the bed in such a position that she could watch her friend, while appearing to be herself asleep.

Before many minutes had passed, she saw, from between half-closed eyelashes, that Mrs. Dale was sitting up, and bending her head in a listening attitude. And presently the slender figure with its white dressing-gown slipped softly off the sofa, and hurried on tiptoe across the floor to the door. There it knelt down and listened again. And after a few minutes Mrs. Dale turned the key in the lock and crept back, not to the couch, but to the arm-chair.

Mabin shut her eyes and tried to disentangle the knot of strange ideas that filled her brain:

What was the nature of the secret which weighed on the conscience of Mrs. Dale? Why was she kept in luxury by the very woman who tried to make her life unbearable, to cut her off from every human friend? What was the strange tie between the hard, elderly woman and the impulsive, volatile young one? What was the vision which had caused her so much distress? And, above all, why, if it was only a vision, did she try to keep it away by locking the door?

And why—and why—? More questions surged up into her tired brain; but Mabin forgot them as they rose. She fell asleep.

When she awoke in the morning it was to find that some one was knocking at the door, and then she heard the housemaid's voice announcing that it was eight o'clock. She sprang up, and looked toward the sofa, but there was no one but herself in the room.

Surely, she thought, the strange visit of the night must have been a dream? The rug on the sofa was neatly folded, just as it had been when she came up to bed last night. Not a sign was to be seen of any intrusion during the night.

Even when she went downstairs and met Mrs. Dale in the hall, there was little to tell of the experience of the hours of darkness. Perhaps the pretty widow looked a little paler than usual, but in every other respect she was the same airy, impulsive creature, now smiling, now looking sad, as she had been before the dreadful visit of the lady whom irreverent Mabin called "the cat."

It was not indeed until breakfast was over and they had gone out into the garden to cut some flowers while the dew was on them, that either of the ladies made any reference to the events of the night.

Mrs. Dale, with one daintily shod foot in a flower-bed, was stretching out her hands toward a bush of sweet-peas, when, without turning her head, she said:

"I am in great trouble about you, Mabin."

"Are you? Why, Mrs. Dale?"

"I don't quite know what to do with you. If I send you to Mrs. Bonnington, I shall have to tell some shocking tarradiddle about the drains having come up, or the roof having given way, and she will be sure to find me out and to pry, and to give both of us what the old women call 'much unpleasantness.' And if I send you on to Geneva, I don't know whether they will be glad to see you when you arrive."

"And I'm sure they won't," said Mabin heartily. "And there is one other objection to sending me anywhere, and that is that I won't go."

Mrs. Dale dropped her sweet-peas, and turned round. Her eyes were full of sudden tears.

"Nonsense, child!" she said sharply, but in a querulous tone which betrayed her emotion, "nonsense! It was decided yesterday afternoon that you were to go. You know it was."

"You decided that I was to go. *I* didn't. And—" instinctively she dropped her voice—"And something that happened last night—in the night, made *me* decide not to go. There!"

"But, my dear——"

"No, Mrs. Dale, I'm not to be 'got round.' You've chosen to take me upon your shoulders, so now you must just keep me. Ha, ha! You didn't know I had so much determination, did you?"

But Mrs. Dale could scarcely speak. Now for the first time that morning Mabin realized that the scene of the night had really taken place, for the emotion aroused by this little bit of talk had brought back into Mrs. Dale's blue eyes a faint reproduction of the wild terror she had shown when she came to the girl's room. When she had recovered her voice, the lady in black, pale, hoarse, shaken with her agitation, stammered out these words:

"My dear girl, it is beautiful of you to offer to stay. But I cannot let you. You ought never to have come. I was mad, wicked to let you come; and my madness and my wickedness I must bear alone."

How strange these words seemed in the broad daylight, Mabin thought! By the weak glimmer of the night-light Mrs. Dale's wild looks and words had seemed fantastic, weird. But the broad sunlight seemed to give the nameless horror which hung about the poor little lady in black a reality as vivid as it was painful. But with this feeling there came also into the heart of the young girl a great tenderness toward the suffering woman, who was haunted by the shadow of her own past. So she smiled, and with a pretty, half-shy look in her eyes, said:

"You told me I saved you from going mad. So I mean to stay. And I mean to sleep in the same room with you, so that you shall not be frightened any more."

Mrs. Dale shook her head.

"I can't let you do that," said she. "I don't sleep very well, and sometimes I start up and cry out. I should frighten you."

"Then we will exchange rooms," said Mabin.

By the look of joy and relief which flashed over Mrs. Dale's face at this suggestion, Mabin saw that she had conquered.

"But—won't you be afraid?" asked the widow in a troubled voice.

"What! Of a ghost, a vision? Or of having bad dreams? No, not a bit."

Mrs. Dale glanced gratefully at the young face, with its look of robust Philistine scorn of phantoms.

"It is a temptation," she murmured. "For, after all, I know, I *know* that it was only a dream, a horrible dream. And there is no fear that the dream will come to *you*."

"And if it did," retorted Mabin stoutly, "it wouldn't frighten me. I'm too 'stodgy;' I have no imagination."

Mrs. Dale smiled sadly.

"You are right," she said. "If you did have the same dream, it would have no terrors for you. Your conscience is clear."

"And my digestion good," added Mabin lightly, as she picked up the fallen flowers and put them in her basket.

There was no doubt that her refusal to go had taken a load of melancholy from the shoulders of her hostess, who sent the young girl out for a walk as soon as the gathering of the flowers was over, and charged her not to go far enough to tire her still weak ankle.

Mabin, with a book and a sunshade, sauntered slowly down the hill to the nearest gap in the cliff, and went down the steep descent to the sands. This was no paradise of nursemaids and babies, but a solitary nook beloved by quiet maiden ladies and sentimental couples. With rash disregard of the danger of sitting under a chalk cliff, Mabin found a seat on a rock worn smooth by the sea, opened her book and began—*not* to read.

The circumstances to which she found herself were far too interesting for her to be able to give herself up to the milder excitements of fiction. She sat with her open book on her lap and her eyes staring out at the sea, which was vividly blue in the strong sunshine, when she became suddenly conscious of a footstep she knew in her immediate neighborhood.

Although she affected to be surprised when Rudolph appeared before her, she had known that he was approaching, and her heart began to beat very fast. He looked down at her between the spikes of her sunshade, pretending to be afraid to speak to her.

"Good-morning," said she at last.

"I was wondering whether I dared say the same thing!"

"Dared?"

"Yes. After your treatment of me last night, I felt nervous."

"My treatment of you! What treatment?"

"Why were you so unkind? Or mustn't I ask why?"

"You may ask, of course. But I can't give you any answer, because I didn't know that I was unkind."

"I wish I could believe that."

"Well, if you won't believe it, I have nothing to say."

Rudolph was silent a few minutes. Then with a burst of explosive energy, he made up his mind.

"No!" he cried so loudly that Mabin started, and threw himself down on the sand beside her, "I will not be daunted. I will encase myself in double snub-proof armor plates, and I will try to teach her that to be dignified it is not necessary to be unkind—and—yes, I will say it—absolutely rude."

Mabin became crimson, and the tears started to her eyes. She had not meant to be rude, but undoubtedly her behavior had laid her open to this accusation.

"I am stupid, clumsy; I am rude without meaning it," she said in a tone of such excessive humility and penitence that it was impossible to doubt her sincerity. "I am very sorry. But you shouldn't take any notice of what I do or say. Nobody does at home. When I am more awkward and tiresome than usual, they always say: 'Oh, it's only Mabin!' And then nobody minds."

"Ah, well, I can't quite feel like that—that it's only Mabin. When one likes a person, and wants to be good friends, very good friends with that person, just as one used to be when that person and one's self were little things in short frocks and knickerbockers, it is very disheartening to find that person so determined to be—er—to be—er—so reserved that when one sits beside that person as I did last night, you know, she will only let one see so much of her right ear as to practically turn her back to one!"

"I didn't!"

"You did though. And it is what you were doing again just now until the horror of hearing the truth made you turn around to fly at me! You did turn your back upon me last night, Miss Rose, and you hurt my feelings."

"Indeed, you did not seem to be hurt. You seemed to be enjoying yourself very much!"

"Well, so I was in a way. But I should have enjoyed myself much more if you had been as nice as you were in the garden."

Mabin heaved a deep sigh.

"It's no use expecting me to be nice," she said in a voice of despair, "I can only manage it so very seldom."

"Well, could you hold out some signal, such as by wearing a particular flower, or color, or some especial knot of ribbon, to let one know when one may speak to you without being snubbed?"

"No, I couldn't," retorted Mabin with great fierceness, but with a twinkle of fun in her gray eyes, which gave greater hopes than her words did. "It is of no use for me to promise more than I can perform. You had much better look upon me as a decidedly disagreeable person, with rare moments of proper behavior."

"Proper behavior, then, means niceness? I'm glad you think it proper to be nice to me!" said Rudolph. "I perceive that I've lighted upon one of the 'rare moments,' and I'm going to take advantage of it," he added, as he came a little nearer to her, and looked up in her face with a glance of amusement and admiration which made her blush a little. "I'm going to make you talk to me, and amuse me, as you were told to do last night."

"No! It was *you* who were told to amuse me!"

"Was it? Well, we'll take it in turn then. Do you remember how I taught you cricket?"

"Yes, oh yes."

"And what a rage you used to be in when you were caught out?"

"Yes," answered Mabin, "I remember; but I don't want to talk about cricket. I want to tell you something. Mrs. Dale has a fancy that 'The Towers' is haunted."

And she related the adventure of the previous night, and her intention of changing rooms with her hostess.

Rudolph listened gravely, and there was a pause when she had finished before he made any comment. Then he said abruptly:

"You are not nervous, are you, Mabin? I know you used to have no end of pluck."

"Well, I haven't any less than I ever had."

"Well, if you do change rooms, you have got to be prepared to see the ghost yourself."

"You make me feel rather—rather creepy! What do you really think I shall see?"

"A face at the window probably. The face of the spy from your house. What else can she have seen?"

Mabin considered a moment.

"I'll risk it!" she cried at last. "I shan't go to bed at all. I shall sit up and watch."

"I wish you would. We should find out something if you had the strength of mind to do that."

Not without a wild beating of the heart, Mabin undertook the task of holding the strange night-watch, without saying a word to Mrs. Dale of her intention.

"She thinks she only had a dreadful dream, you know," said Mabin.

"Well," replied Rudolph, "I want to know what sort of dream you will have."

He had to admire the courage she showed in undertaking a task which was, as she expressed it, "rather shuddery," but when he left her at the gate of "The Towers" she was still steadfast in her intention.

It was not until after dinner that evening that Mrs. Dale introduced the young girl to the apartment she was to occupy that night. Mabin was astonished at its dinginess, its gloominess, contrasting so strongly as they did with the fresh prettiness of the room which had been prepared for herself.

It was a large square room, with a mouldy old-fashioned wall-paper, on which unnatural pink roses climbed up a succession of thin hop poles. The pictures were groups of trees, done with the pencil in the woolly early Victorian manner, and stiff bouquets, in water-color, of conventional early Victorian flowers. The bed, which was hung with green curtains, occupied an undue space; and Mabin felt that, in the weird circumstances of her tenancy of the room, she would have died rather than sleep in that funereal erection.

When Mrs. Dale had kissed her and bade her good-night, after receiving Mabin's assurance that she did not feel in the least nervous, the young girl felt a strong inclination to follow her friend out of the room, and to implore her to find her some other sleeping-place.

By a valiant effort, however, she conquered this weakness, and made a careful survey of her surroundings. In the first place, the windows and their fastenings had to be examined. They were carefully secured, and were both so high above the ground that it would have been impossible for an intruder to reach them without a ladder.

There were three doors; and at first Mabin was inclined to regard this as a disquieting circumstance. But on finding that two of them were unused, locked, and without a key, and that there was a bolt on the door by which she had entered, she began to feel more at ease.

Exchanging her frock for a dressing-gown, and providing herself with a book, she placed herself in an arm-chair which stood near the fireplace, which, although shabby, was sufficiently comfortable, and, putting her candles on a small table beside her, settled herself to read. Her book was a novel of an excellent type, not too clever to be charming, not so commonplace as to be dull. Much to her own surprise, she got interested, and forgot, or almost forgot, the vague fears which kept her in the arm-chair instead of in bed.

She was in the very heart of the book, and her candles had burnt low in their sockets, when a sound, a very slight sound, behind her back, caused the blood almost to freeze in her veins.

It was a soft, stealthy tread.

Looking round, half paralyzed with terror, she saw that the door was ajar, and that creeping softly round toward the inside handle was the long, thin hand of a man.

CHAPTER IX.
A PICTURE.

IN the ordinary course of things, it would have been natural for Mabin to conclude, on seeing a man's hand inside her door in the middle of the night, that the intruder was a burglar. But her mind had been rendered more clear, her perceptions more acute, by the stimulating mystery which she had been for the past two days trying to solve.

Instead, therefore, of screaming, or stretching out her hand to the old-fashioned bell-rope which hung by the fireside at a little distance from her right hand, she waited, watched, and listened. Apparently she had unconsciously made some slight noise as she turned in her chair to look behind her, for the intruder, whoever he was, instead of entering, waited and listened also.

There was a pause; and then the hand which had crept so stealthily round the door was slowly and quietly withdrawn. Mabin, fascinated, watched the long, bloodless fingers as they gradually disappeared from her sight; and was sufficiently self-possessed to observe that the hand was that of a gentleman. And upon this discovery there sprang up in her mind a strong curiosity to see the face of the intruder.

Even while she felt the last remains of fear give place to courage and vivid interest, Mabin, with her wits all sharpened with excitement, wondered at the change in herself. She sprang lightly to her feet, and with the intention of taking him by surprise, ran lightly round on the tips of her toes toward the door. But the candles, flickering in the draught caused by her light hanging sleeves, caused the shadows on the dingy rose-covered wall to dance and quiver. The mysterious visitor, as much on the alert as the girl was, closed the door softly between her and himself.

Mabin, however, sprang forward and seized the door-handle. She heard the sound of rapid footsteps on the other side, and for one moment she hesitated to go in pursuit. With the clearness of intellect which belongs to the night, when there are no sounds of busy life, no distractions of bright light and vivid color to divert the attention, she saw both the dangers on the one hand, the attractions on the other, of a deeper dive into the mystery which surrounded her. For a few seconds the impulses struggled against each other, and then curiosity and youthful daring carried the day.

Throwing open the door, which had not been relocked, and in which there was no key, Mabin, considering this circumstance as she went, dashed through in pursuit.

It was indeed a daring thing to do, for she was not even mistress of the topography of the house. The room in which she now found herself she had never been in before, and the only light to guide her footsteps came through the window and was obscured by a yellow-white blind. It was by this light that Mabin knew that the dawn had come, and the knowledge gave her more courage. She could follow the intruder with greater security now that she knew that, if she chased him to the place where he had entered the house, she would see his face in the daylight.

As she entered the room the man was in the act of opening a door on the left which led into the corridor. Mabin saw him for a moment, against the brighter light which came through the windows on the east side of the house; and then this door closed between her and him as the other had done.

By the time she had got into the corridor in her turn, she saw the man disappear down the stairs at the end. She followed still. He reached the hall; he went down the four steps to the drawing-room, through the doorway of which he again passed out of her sight.

In the midst of the excitement which hurried her on to the drawing-room door, the young girl felt a chill in her blood as she remembered Mrs. Dale's description of the gloom of the deserted apartment. She had described it as "a damp and mouldy mausoleum." Mabin would have avoided the room if she could. The meeting with her mysterious visitor would be more uncanny there than in the warmer, more habitable parts of the house.

But she went on. Dashing into the room with impetuosity all the greater for her vague fears, Mabin found herself in a very long, wide, low-ceilinged room, the roof of which was supported by two rows of pillars, and the air of which struck a chill into her.

There were three large windows, two on the right hand, and one at the end of the room, in front of her. Above the shutters of those on her right the gray rays of the morning were creeping, making the marble of the heavy old mantelpiece look livid, and showing the stains of damp on the white and gold wall-paper.

This was all that the girl had time to notice when suddenly the shutters of the window at the end of the room were thrown back with a clatter of wood and a clang of iron, and she saw the green of the trees outside, and the man of whom she was in pursuit standing in the opening he had made. And then she saw that the French window was open, and knew that this was the way by which he had entered the house.

The word "Stop!" was on her lips when suddenly he seemed to stagger, and she heard him gasp and struggle for his breath. Surely this was no burglar, this man with the thin white hands, who could not run a distance of a hundred yards without inconvenience.

She tumbled over a footstool, and as she drew herself up again, she saw that she was alone in the room.

Running lightly and quickly to the window she looked out into the garden. The fresh morning breeze blew the open window against the wooden shutter with a loud crash. At the same moment she caught sight of the figure of which she had been in pursuit so long, under the trees to the right. At the noise of the crashing window the man turned quickly round, and in the pale light of the dawn Mabin saw his face distinctly.

In a moment the last trace of fear of him which had lingered in her heart disappeared. Almost as pale as a mask of the dead, the face she saw was that of a man on whom every form of suffering seemed to have left its mark. The hollow eyes were full of unspeakable sadness; the deep lines about the mouth were those of illness or sorrow rather than of age; while even the thick sprinkling of gray hairs among the brown which Mabin detected in the searching cold light of the morning told the same tale of weight of grief rather than of years.

All these things the girl's quick young eyes saw in one brief look. Then, instinctively, she took a step forward into the garden, with some vague intention of asking him a question. But the moment she moved he turned; and disappearing from her sight behind the trees and shrubs which grew between the lawn and the spot where she stood, left her in a state of surprise and bewilderment from which it took her some minutes to recover.

It was the physical fact that she began to shiver violently in the keen morning air which at last roused her from the dazed condition into which the chase and its end had thrown her. She got into the house again, shut the window, fastened the shutter carefully, wondering by what magical means it had been opened from the outside, and stumbled along the musty drawing-room in the half-light until she reached the door.

Opening it quickly, she caught sight of Annie, the housemaid, rapidly turning the corner of the staircase above. With suspicion in her mind, she called the girl; but Annie disappeared into the upper regions of the house, paying no attention to her.

Uneasy, interested, puzzled, Mabin went slowly upstairs, started violently when the tall clock on the stairs struck four close to her ear, and stood before the open door of the room through which the intruder had passed on his way to and from hers.

Who was this man with the grave, sad, handsome face, who got into the house by night, and stole his way to the very bed-chamber of Mrs. Dale? In what relation did he stand to the lovely widow?

No honest man, whether relation, friend, or lover, would pay his mysterious visits like these! And yet there was something in his face so attractive, so interesting, that Mabin would fain have believed that there was some reason, some excuse, for his strange conduct. And the one excuse which she unwillingly had to find was this: the man must be mad.

This began to show a way out of the mystery; but it was by no means cleared up. Was he the man who had taken her father's house as "Mr. Banks"? This seemed probable, and at any rate this could be easily ascertained. If so, and if "Mr. Banks" was a madman, why was he unattended by any keeper?

And what, "Mr. Banks" or no "Mr. Banks," was the meaning of these stealthy nocturnal visits? That they were so unexpected, so unwelcome, as to be inconceivable on the part of Mrs. Dale, had been abundantly proved by the fact that she had believed the visitor to be a vision of her imagination only, and not a human being. For Mabin could not doubt that the appearance which Mrs. Dale had taken for a horrible dream had been in reality the living man she had just seen.

Who then could he be, and what could he want? Was the refined, sensitive face, with its sad eyes and worn mouth, the mask and not the index of the man?

The more Mabin thought, the clearer it seemed to grow to her that the man was either a relation or a lover, who had gone out of his mind, and whose insanity had taken this strange form of nocturnal persecution.

But then, again, if he had been insane, would not Mrs. Dale have heard of it? And was it not rather the act of a sane man than of a madman to assume a name not his own in order to hide his identity from the woman he meant to harass? Again, was the intruder the tenant of "Stone House" at all?

Even of this she was not sure; and Mabin decided that this question must be answered definitely before she could think herself on the road to the discovery of the mystery.

In the mean time, the door of the room through which she had passed in pursuit of the intruder being still open, she entered, and instinctively looked round, to see if he had left any trace of his presence.

She drew up the blind and let the daylight stream into the corners.

The room was like the rest of the house, shabby and furnished with little taste. It had perhaps been a study or a school-room, for in front of the one window there was a large leather-covered writing-table, much splashed with ink. The rest of the furniture consisted of a couple of small ottomans and half a dozen chairs, all covered with green rep, and trimmed with green worsted fringe, and of a mahogany bookcase which stood near the door.

Mabin, with one glance round, had satisfied herself that nothing in the room betrayed the recent presence of an intruder, when her attention was suddenly arrested by a picture on the wall to her left.

It was a portrait in oils of a man, very young, very handsome, and bearing, as she saw at once, a great resemblance to the man she had seen a quarter of an hour before escaping from the house.

A great resemblance, that was all; it did not occur to her for some minutes that the man in the picture and the man she had seen could be the same person. But as her fascinated eyes pored over the painting, studying each feature, it grew upon her gradually that the likeness between it and the man was that of a face in happiness to a face in sorrow, and she saw the possibility that they were one and the same person.

As this thought crossed her mind, she stepped back startled by her own discovery. The light, growing stronger every moment, began to bathe the picture in the brightness of a summer morning, and she noticed then with what care it had been preserved. A tiny rod ran along the top of the picture, and from it hung two curtains, now drawn aside, of dark blue satin, hung with bullion fringe, and embroidered richly in shades of blue and gold.

Mabin's eyes, attracted by the beautiful colors, were fixed upon this handsome hanging, when a piercing cry, uttered by a voice she did not recognize, but which thrilled her by its wild grief, made her start and turn round.

Just within the door by which she had entered the room Mrs. Dale was lying prone, motionless, on the floor.

Mabin, trembling from head to foot, went down on her knees beside her friend, and found that she had fainted. Not wishing to call the servants, she ran into the adjoining bedroom, fetched some water, and sprinkled it on the face of the unconscious woman. But at first Mrs. Dale gave no sign of life, and Mabin had time to reflect on the course she had better take.

And as, she thought, Mrs. Dale's sudden loss of consciousness must be in some way connected with the picture, it would be better that she should find herself, on recovering, in another room.

Mabin was so much taller than Mrs. Dale that she found it a comparatively easy task to drag the little, slenderly made creature into the adjoining bedroom, and when she got her upon the sofa at the foot of the bed she found that the pink color was returning to her patient's cheeks, that her hands and eyelids were moving slightly, and that a sigh was struggling up to her lips.

"Do you feel better now, dear?" asked Mabin rather tremulously.

For she had some doubts as to the scene which might be impending.

Mrs. Dale opened her eyes, but made no answer. She did not seem to hear Mabin; she seemed to be listening, trying to remember.

"Would you like a little water?" went on Mabin, rather frightened by the silence, and betraying her feelings in her tone and in the expression of her face. Then Mrs. Dale sat up, and the rather vacant look on her face grew into one of weary sadness.

"No, dear, thank you. I am not thirsty; and I—and I—am quite well."

As she said this she rose, and glanced anxiously round the room. Then she looked at the door which communicated with the adjoining apartment, and suddenly sprang toward it.

"Don't, don't go in there!" cried Mabin, quickly, imploringly.

Mrs. Dale, with a deadly white face, stopped short, turned and looked at her.

"Why not?" she asked abruptly, in a whisper.

"Why, because—because—" stammered the girl, "it was in there you fainted. Don't you remember?"

She took one of Mrs. Dale's ice-cold hands in her own, in the hope of communicating the warmth of her own young blood to her terror-stricken friend.

"I—I remember. I found you looking——"

She broke off suddenly, snatched her hand from the girl's, and ran into the next room. Mabin followed hesitatingly, and found her standing in front of the picture, with her eyes fixed upon it. Mabin said nothing, afraid lest by some unlucky word she should increase the mental distress of the unhappy woman. She uttered a cry as Mrs. Dale, turning upon her fiercely, asked in a tone which she had never used to her before:

"Why did you come in here? And what made you draw back the curtains?" Then evidently regretting her violence of manner when she saw how strong an effect it had upon the girl, she added with an abrupt change to apologetic gentleness, and with tears of penitence in her eyes: "I beg your pardon, dear; but—but it is not like you to be so curious."

Mabin hesitated. She did not dare to tell Mrs. Dale what it was that had brought her into the room. For, she argued to herself, if the mere sight of this man's portrait, and the belief that she had only dreamed she saw him, had such an effect upon the little woman, what might not the result be of finding that he had been there in the flesh?

"The door was open," she said at last.

And she felt quite glad that Mrs. Dale evidently doubted her word, and looked again in a puzzled manner at the portrait.

"What made you draw back the curtains?" was her next question.

"I didn't. I found the picture like that. I haven't touched it," answered Mabin quickly and rather indignantly.

But her transitory anger passed away when she saw the change to deep trouble which instantly took place in Mrs. Dale's face. Putting up her handkerchief with shaking fingers to her wet, white face, the little lady clung with the other hand to the old writing-table, by which she was standing. She was in a state of great agitation, but Mabin did not know whether she ought to appear to be conscious of the fact or not. At last Mrs. Dale asked, in a hoarse whisper:

"That noise—I heard a noise in the house—and Annie, I saw Annie running upstairs—What was it?"

"The drawing-room window had been left open and it banged against the shutter," replied Mabin. "I went down and shut it, and Annie went down too."

She was ashamed to have to make this equivocal answer, but she dared not tell the whole truth—yet. She must have more of her friend's confidence first, she must know more. And again she asked herself whether this man was some old lover of Mrs. Dale's, who had been shut up on account of insanity, and of whose confinement Mrs. Dale had heard. She thought she would make an attempt to find out.

"What a handsome face this is!" she said, controlling her own nervous agitation as well as she could, and fixing her gaze upon the picture. "I don't think I ever saw a face I admired so much."

There was a pause, and Mabin, without looking round, heard her companion draw a deep breath. Presently, however, the latter recovered her self-possession sufficiently to ask, with an assumption of her usual playful tone:

"Not—Rudolph's?"

Mabin was taken completely off her guard. Her mind filled with the story of her friend, she had for the time forgotten her own.

"Oh, that is a different type of face, quite different," she replied, relapsing at once into the formal tone of the shy school-girl.

"But not without its good points?" suggested Mrs. Dale, coming behind the girl and putting her little hands on her waist.

Mabin, with an inspiration of astuteness, thought she received a short cut to her friend's confidence, a confidence which would clear the ground for further discoveries, further enlightenments.

"Haven't you ever felt that one—person—was outside everything else? And not to be measured by standards at all?" she asked in a soft, shy voice.

Mrs. Dale's answer, the answer, too, of a widow, came upon her like a thunderbolt.

"No, dear. I have had no such experience myself. I have never cared for a man in all my life."

And she spoke with the accents of sincerity.

CHAPTER X.

THE PICKING UP OF SOME SILVER THREADS.

"Mabin!"

"Oh!"

A single syllable hardly conveys the amount of alarm, of horror, of paralyzing fright which Mabin puts into the exclamation.

And yet the occasion was an ordinary one enough. It had simply happened that she had taken her work to the old seat at the edge of the plantation, where the primitive picnics used to take place in the old days, and that Rudolph had come up softly over the fields without her hearing his footsteps on the yielding grass.

"I frightened you?"

"N—no, not exactly, but you made me drop my needle. I thought you were at Portsmouth!"

"So I was. But that isn't five thousand miles off. I came back this morning."

Mabin said nothing. She had not seen him for a fortnight,—not, in fact, since the morning when he had met her on the seashore, and when he had applauded her resolution of sleeping in the room in which Mrs. Dale had had her bad dream. He had been called away suddenly on the following day, and had therefore heard nothing of Mabin's adventure.

"Haven't you got any news for me? I had rather expected a budget."

Now Mabin had a budget for him, and had been looking forward most anxiously for his return, that she might confide in him some of the suspicions, the surmises, which filled her brain by day, and even kept her awake at night. But as usual with events long looked forward to, this return of Rudolph's had not taken place as she expected, and she found herself in a state of unreadiness to meet him.

In the first place, she felt so ridiculously excited, so absurdly glad, that all the things she had been storing up in her mind to tell him dwindled into sudden insignificance. What did they matter, what did anything matter just now, except that Rudolph had come back, and that she must try not to let him guess how glad she was?

"Yes," she said deliberately, after a short pause, looking across the clover field to the sea, and carefully choosing another needle, "I have plenty to tell you. I had it all ready, but—but you came up so suddenly that you have scattered all the threads of the story, and now I don't remember where to begin."

"I'm so awfully sorry. First you say I make you lose your needle, and then I scatter your threads. I'm afraid you think me in the way."

No answer.

"Must I go?"

Rudolph got up and drew back a step, standing in the long, rank grass which bordered the clover field in the shade of the trees of the plantation.

"If I say yes, I suppose you will say I'm being rude again!" said Mabin, as she threw up at him, from under her big shady hat, a shy glance so full of attraction in its unconscious coquetry that Rudolph also forgot the budget, and thought he had never seen any girl look half so pretty as she did.

"I should say," said he, bending his head as he spoke, and looking with great apparent interest at the work in her hands, "that you were unkind."

There was another pause. Never before, even in the days of her wooden shyness, had Mabin found speech with him so difficult. A lump seemed to rise in her throat whenever she had a remark ready, and for fear of betraying the fact she remained silent altogether.

It was odd, too, that Rudolph, who had always been so fluent of speech himself, and had made her seem so dull, had now become infected with her own stupid reticence.

"You are a long time finding one," said he at last.

"Yes. I—I seem to have lost all the fine ones," replied Mabin, bending her head still lower than before over her needle case.

"Let me help you. Give me the work first, so that I can judge what size you want."

"How can you tell—a man?" asked Mabin with indignation.

And in her contempt she looked up at him again.

"Oh-ho, madam! Don't you know that we sailors can use a needle as well as any woman. Here let me show you."

This was an admirable opportunity for seating himself on the bench beside her; and Rudolph, who had felt a strange hesitation about doing so before, now took the plunge, and placed himself on the end of the wooden seat.

"What is this? An antimacassar?"

"No. A cooking apron."

"How interesting! Ladies ought not to make such things. They should do things that want lots of bundles of silks of all sorts of colors. This isn't sufficiently decorative."

"You mean fancy-work!" exclaimed Mabin with an expression of horror. "I hate fancy-work!"

"Girls who do fancy-work can always give a fellow things they have made themselves to remember them by. I have a heap of tobacco pouches, all very pretty and too good to use. Now you couldn't give a fellow a cooking apron, to remember you by, could you?"

"I shouldn't want anybody to remember me—with a lot of other girls!" retorted Mabin fiercely.

And then she felt the blood rush to her cheeks, and she thrust the needle-case quickly into his hands.

"Find one now, find one!" cried she imperiously, "and let me see what you can do. I believe you are only boasting when you say you can sew."

Rudolph took the apron from her, and the needle-case, found a needle of the size he wanted in half the time she had spent in searching for one, and took up her hem where she had left off, working with fine, even stitches which called forth her unwilling admiration.

"Why," she cried, in great surprise, "you do it beautifully! It's better than mine!"

"Of course it is," remarked Rudolph calmly. "Whatever the superior sex does bears, of course, the mark of superiority. The only thing that women can do really well is to receive prettily the attentions of the sex, it is useless for them to try to emulate. You used to do it very well once. I am hoping you haven't lost the knack."

"You haven't lost your old knack of conceit, I see."

"Oh, no. I have just the same opinion of myself and just the same opinion of you as when you used to send me wading into the pools between the rocks to get little crabs for you, and into the hedges for bird's eggs, one from each nest, don't you remember? And when you used to make me so proud by saying I found them quicker than anybody else. And then—do you remember what you used to do then?"

"Break them on the way home, I suppose," said she, trying to look as if she had forgotten.

"Come, don't you really remember any better than that?"

He had finished his needleful of thread, and handed her back the apron. So that he was at leisure to watch her face as she folded the big piece of holland, and collected the odds and ends of her work-bag. And it was quite clear to him that her memory was as true as his.

"Don't you remember that you always gave me a kiss when I found a robin's nest?"

"No, indeed, I don't."

But she did. Eyes, cheeks, and mouth all betrayed the scandalizing recollection.

"And used to promise to marry me when you grew up? Now, do you mean to say you've forgotten that?"

Evidently loss of memory was no protection with this person. Mabin blushed, and tried another sort of answer.

"Yes, I remember. What funny things children say!"

"Was it—funny?"

71

"Why, yes, I can't help laughing at the idea now!"

And Mabin began to laugh hysterically, unnaturally, but withal so prettily, with so much of maidenly confusion and subdued happiness mingling with her amusement, that Rudolph threw his arm round her in the midst of her mirth, and cut it short by snatching a kiss.

"Oh!"

The monosyllable was meant to express astonishment and indignation, but it was a poor little protest after all, and one of which Rudolph did not feel bound to take much notice.

"Are you angry?" said he, not withdrawing his arm. "Are you very angry, Mabin? Don't you think you will ever be able to forgive me?"

"I am angry, certainly," answered she, trying to release herself. "I hope you are going to apologize for—for forgetting that I am not nine now."

"How old are you, Mabin?"

"Nineteen."

"Quite old enough to take up the promises you made ten years ago. Quite old enough to marry me."

"Rudolph! What nonsense!"

"Oh, is it nonsense? If you think I'm going to allow my feelings to be trifled with by a chit of a girl who used to go halves with me in bull's eyes, you're very much mistaken! Now then, are you willing to ratify your promise, or am I to bring an action for breach?"

But Mabin, trembling with excitement and happiness so great as to be bewildering, felt dimly that there was too much levity about this abrupt settlement of the affairs of two lifetimes. This sudden proposal did not accord with her serious disposition, with her sense of the fitness of things. She looked at him with eyes pathetically full of something like terror.

"Rudolph!" she whispered, in a voice which was unsteady with strong emotion, "how can you talk like this? How can you? Don't you know that *it hurts*?"

"Hurts, little one? What do you mean by that?"

His tone was tender enough to satisfy the most exacting damsel, but Mabin was struck with fresh terror on remarking that instead of releasing her he tightened the grasp in which he held her.

"Why, I mean—I mean—that you are in play, that, it is amusement, fun, to you; while to me—"

And then she saw in his eyes something new, something of the earnestness, the seriousness which she had longed for, but which she had not before detected in the light-hearted sailor.

"While to you—? Why, little one, do you think it is anything to you, this promise that I am to have you to guard and to keep near my heart for our lives, more than it is to me? Do you think one must meet one's happiness with a sour face, Mabin, and ask a girl to love you from the other side of a stone wall? Oh, my little sweetheart, with the shy eyes and the proud heart, you have a great deal to learn; and the very first thing is to trust me, and not to think my love of no account because I can woo you with a light heart."

Every word seemed to echo in the young girl's heart. She was taken off her feet, lifted high into an enchanted region where words were music, and a touch of the fingers ecstasy, and she hardly dared to speak, to move, to draw breath lest the spell should be broken, and she should wake up to commonplace life again. She listened, hardly speaking, to her lover as he told her how she had always remained in his mind as the childish figure that foreshadowed his womanly ideal; how her cold reserve had piqued him, made him study her the more; and finally how quickly these feelings had given place to warmer ones when he and she became friends once more.

They did not know how the time went. The sun rose high, the shadows shifted gradually, the dew dried on the long grass. At last a bell, ringing loudly in the garden behind the plantation, startled Mabin, and made her spring up.

"That's for luncheon, it must be for luncheon!" she cried in blushing confusion. "I'd forgotten—forgotten everything!"

Rudolph laughed gently, and picked up her bag and her work.

"I won't come in," said he. "But I'll go through the plantation with you to carry these."

Across Mabin's face there came a cloud.

"You must see Mrs. Dale," she said. "She will want to see you, and yet——"

"And yet what?"

"I'm jealous."

"Are you? For shame, for shame! Can't you trust me?"

"I will say yes, of course, but——"

"But you mean no. Well, I can promise not to break your heart."

And he laughed at her and teased her, and told her that Mrs. Dale was too well off to trouble her head about a poor lieutenant.

But Mabin was only half comforted; she remembered how well they had got on together on that memorable evening when a misunderstanding had caused her to sulk, and she was too diffident to believe that her own charms could compete with brilliant Mrs. Dale's.

As soon as they came out of the plantation, and within sight of the house, they saw across the lawn the young housemaid, Annie, shading her eyes with her hand, as if watching for some one. Mabin, thinking the girl was looking out for her, sprang away from Rudolph, calling out a last "Good-by" as she hurried over the lawn.

"Tell Mrs. Dale that I am coming to call upon her this afternoon, to ask her to give me some tea. And please remind her that she promised me peaches next time I came," called out Rudolph after her as she ran.

Mabin merely waved her hand to imply that she heard, and ran on toward the house. Annie, instead of retreating into the hall at the approach of the young lady, stepped out into the garden. And when Rudolph, after skirting the plantation, reached the gravelled space on his way to the gate, he found the young housemaid holding it open for him. He saw, before he came up, by the girl's look and manner that she had something to say to him.

"I beg your pardon, sir," she said in a low voice, as soon as he was near enough to hear, "but I hope you won't mind me taking the liberty of speaking to you."

The girl was a bright-looking young person, with intelligent eyes and an open, pleasant face.

"Well, what is the portentous secret?" asked Rudolph, smiling, much amused by her assumed airs of mystery and importance.

"Well, sir, it is a secret," she retorted, rather nettled by his amusement. "It's a warning I have to give you, sir."

"A warning! Come, this begins to be interesting."

"It isn't a joke at all, sir," said the housemaid, half offended, yet with increasing earnestness. "I saw you coming over the field this morning, sir, when I was out speaking to the gardener about the salad. And I thought you was most likely coming here, sir, and I've been on the lookout for you ever since."

"Much obliged to you, I'm sure. But have you been told to warn me off the premises?"

The girl drew herself up.

"Well, I can tell you, sir, that you'd better not come about the place more than you can help, for if you do there's some one that will find it out and maybe do you a mischief. Hoping you'll excuse the liberty, sir; but I know something nobody else does, and I shouldn't like you to come to any harm, sir."

And leaving Rudolph in a state of mingled incredulity, amusement, and surprise, the girl shut the gate, through which he had by this time passed, ran back quickly and disappeared through the back door into the house.

It was with a shock that Mabin remembered, when she met Mrs. Dale, that in the excitement of her own happiness she had neglected to tell Rudolph the story of her midnight adventure. This remembrance filled the girl with compunction. She reproached herself with thinking of no one but herself, and was as miserable over her omission as she had been happy while with her lover. As it was in the dining-room that she met Mrs. Dale, the presence of the parlormaid prevented her from confiding to her friend's ear the events of the morning. She said with a hot blush that she had met Rudolph and gave his message; but although Mrs. Dale received the intelligence with an arch smile she did not guess how extremely interesting the interview had proved.

And as after luncheon Mrs. Dale sent her into Seagate for peaches, while she wrote some letters, Mabin kept the secret of her engagement, saving it up until Rudolph should himself break the news.

The young girl felt an odd shyness about confessing her happiness. She was quite glad of the excuse circumstances afforded of keeping it all to herself for a few hours longer. It was a joy so far above all other joys that it seemed to her its bloom would not bear the rough touch of arch words and looks which would certainly follow the announcement of it.

Hugging her happiness to her heart, she went quickly to Seagate and back, not heeding the scorching heat of the sun, or the glare of the chalky roads, or the dust made by the vehicles which passed her on the way. And when she reached "The Towers" again, finding that Mrs. Dale had not yet come downstairs, she put on her hat and went back to the seat where Rudolph had sat with her that morning, to live over again the golden time they had spent there together.

But she could not free her mind from the self-reproach she felt at having forgotten, in the pleasure of the meeting with Rudolph, the affairs of her friend. There was just this excuse for her, that it was now a whole fortnight since the strange night adventure had happened, and during all that time nothing had occurred at "The Towers" to recall the visit of the intruder whom Mabin had chased out of the house. After that strange confidence of Mrs. Dale's, following the incident of the picture, no word more had been exchanged by the two ladies on the subject. It was this new but unavoidable reserve between them which had made Mabin so shy of mentioning her new happiness. If Mrs. Dale had, as she averred, never been in love herself, what sympathy could she be expected to have for Mabin?

With these thoughts in her mind Mabin had at last got up from the seat, and sauntered along the narrow path through the plantation in the direction of her father's house. Crossing the lane which separated the grounds of the two houses, she found herself, without thinking how she came there, on the path which ran along outside the wall at the bottom of her father's garden.

She had gone about ten yards when she heard a slight noise on the inner side of the wall. She stopped. There flashed quickly into her mind the old forgotten question: Was her father's tenant the man who had got into "The Towers" at night a fortnight ago?

Coming noiselessly close to the wall, she reached the top of it by a sudden spring, and saw, between the bushes of the border, the bent figure of a gentleman, sauntering along slowly with the aid of a stick.

The cry she uttered made him look up.

And the face she saw was the face of the picture in the shut-up room, the face of the man she had pursued through the house, whose thin, worn features she had seen a fortnight ago in the pale light of the morning.

CHAPTER XI.
AN INTERVIEW WITH MR. BANKS.

MABIN had only just time to recognize the face of the man who had got into "The Towers" at night as Mr. Banks, her father's tenant, when he turned abruptly and hurried away toward the house.

Mabin's first thought was to get over the wall, a proceeding to which, it must be admitted, she was not unaccustomed, and pursue him, as she had done upon a recent and well-remembered occasion. But she felt a certain natural shyness about such a bold course, and decided that she would proceed in more orthodox fashion by going round to the front door and asking for him.

It was not without fears that she would be unsuccessful that she made her way, slowly and with the slight limp which still remained from her bicycle accident, along the lane to the front of the house. This was the first time she had been inside her father's gates since the morning the family went away, and it struck her with a sense of strangeness that she had lived a great deal faster than ever before since that memorable day. Mrs. Dale's mysterious story; the visit of the old lady with the cruel tongue; the midnight intrusion of Mr. Banks; last, and chief of all, Rudolph's confession of love—these things had opened a wide abyss between the child Mabin and the woman. She felt that she was not the shy girl who had had a nervous dread of leaving home mingling with the thoughts of coming pleasure. And she told herself that when the family came back they would find, not the angular girl they had left, but a woman, a full-fledged woman.

Perhaps she congratulated herself prematurely upon the enormous advance she had made; at any rate, when she rang the bell, she found her heart beating very fast, and a curious feeling rising in her throat which threatened to affect the steadiness of her voice.

It was Langford who opened the door. The old servant had not seen Mabin since the day she had left the house, and her face broke out into smiles as she greeted her.

"Bless me, Miss Mabin, I never thought of its being you! But I am glad to see you. And how have you been getting on? And have you heard from Mrs. Rose lately?"

"I'm getting on splendidly, and I heard from mamma two days ago. Ethel's got the mumps, but the rest are all right. I'll talk to you another time. Come round and see me some evening. Can't you get away? I'm in a hurry now; I want to see Mr. Banks."

Langford shook her head emphatically.

"It's no use wanting that, Miss Mabin. Mr. Banks never sees anybody, not even his lawyer if he can help it. He's a character, he is. Is it a message you've got for him from Mr. Rose?"

"Oh, no. It's something very important, much more important than that. And I must see him; I tell you I *must*! And if you won't help me, I shall go to work in a way of my own, and give the poor man a fright."

"Oh, no, Miss Mabin, you won't do that, I'm sure! You don't know how delicate the poor gentleman is; more than once since he's been here he has given me a fright, and made me think he was going to die. And he's so peculiar; he won't let one send for a doctor, not if it's ever so, he won't. I'm sure one morning, a fortnight ago, when I found him lying on the floor in the hall with the back garden door open, I thought he was dead, that I did. But when I'd brought him to—for he'd fainted, just like a woman—he wouldn't hear of my getting any one to come and see him——"

"Ah!" exclaimed Mabin. "Was that on a Tuesday night—I mean Wednesday morning?"

"Yes, so it was."

Mabin smiled.

"Well, I know the reason of that attack. And perhaps I'll tell you some day, if you'll manage to let me see him now. And first tell me what you think of him. Is he mad, do you think, or what? You remember, when he first came, you thought he was."

Langford shook her head dubiously.

"Well, really, Miss Mabin, I can't rightly tell you what I do think about him. Sometimes I do think he's off his head altogether; he marches up and down the drawing-room—that's the room he has taken to himself—by the hour together, going faster and faster, till I listen outside the door wondering if anything is going to happen, and whether he's going to break out like and do himself a mischief. But if I make an excuse to go in, though his eyes are wide and glaring, so that at the first look he frightens one, yet he always speaks to me quite gently, and says he doesn't want anything. Of course I pretend not to notice anything, and I think he likes the way I take him. For, though he's always civil-spoken to every one, he doesn't let the two girls come near him, if he can help it. If they come up from the kitchen or out of a room when he's by, he just turns his back and waits till they've gone past."

Mabin listened with deep interest, and without interrupting by a question. But when Langford paused for breath, the young girl asked suddenly:

"Does he have any letters? It isn't just curiosity that makes me ask, I needn't tell you."

"No, Miss Mabin. He doesn't have any letters sent here except under cover from his lawyer. They come in big envelopes, with the address stamped on the back, so I know. It looks as if he was in hiding or something, doesn't it?" she added in a discreet whisper.

Mabin thought that it did, and the fact added to the fascination of the mystery.

"You don't think he's a detective, do you?" she whispered close to Langford's ear.

"No, I'm quite sure he isn't. Detectives aren't gentlemen, and Mr. Banks is a gentleman, if ever there was one."

"It's very strange," murmured Mabin vaguely, pondering on the fresh facts.

"You may well say that, Miss Mabin. I don't know what to think myself. Some days he'll sit all day long with his head in his hands without moving scarcely. Or he'll sit poring over what looks like old letters and bits of things that I think must have been a woman's somehow. But there, I feel like a sneak telling these things even to you; for it's only by chance that I know anything about them myself, and for certain Mr. Banks didn't think I should chatter about what I saw."

"Ah, well, I know more than you do as it is," said Mabin softly.

The words were still on her lips when a door opened behind them somewhere in the dark, cool hall, and Mabin started guiltily. She and Langford were standing just within the front doorway, out of hearing of any one in the house. But she forgot that she could not be heard, and felt confused and shy when a man's voice, very low, very gentle, said:

"Langford, is that Miss Rose?"

"Yes, sir," said Langford, as Mabin's eyes at last saw which door it as that was open, and the servant passed her toward the drawing-room.

"I will see her if she wants to speak to me," were his next, most unexpected words.

Mabin entered the drawing-room, and found herself face to face with the mysterious Mr. Banks.

He was standing in the middle of the long room, and as the young lady came in he held out his hand to her and offered her a seat. His hand was cold, his face looked more worn, more gray than ever, and as he moved he tottered, like a man recovering from an illness, or on the verge of one. But Mabin thought, as she looked at him, that her fancy that he must be insane was a mistaken one. It seemed to her now that there was the imprint of a great grief, an ever-present burden of melancholy, upon the grave stranger, but that his straightforward, clear eyes were the sanest she had ever seen.

"You wish to speak to me? To ask me some questions, I suppose?" he said courteously, as he leaned against the mantelpiece and bent his head to listen.

"Yes."

Then there was a pause. It was rather a delicate matter to accuse this grave, courteous gentleman of a burglarious entry into another person's house. Mabin had not felt the full force of this difficulty until now when she sat, breathing quickly, and wondering how to begin, while Mr. Banks still politely waited.

"I saw you just now in the garden," she burst out at last, feeling conscious that her voice sounded coarse and harsh after his quiet tones, "and I recognized you. And I thought it was better to tell you so, to tell you that I knew it was you who—who——"

How could she go on? She didn't. She broke down altogether, and sat looking at the gently stirring branches of the trees outside, wishing that she were under the shelter of their cool freshness, instead of going through this fiery ordeal indoors.

Then it suddenly became clear to her that Mr. Banks had been seized with a new idea.

"I suppose then," he said, and she was delighted to see that he was at last beginning to feel some of the embarrassment which she was suffering, "that you are the lady who followed me through the drawing-room of 'The Towers' a fortnight ago?"

"Yes, yes."

"Then I don't know how to apologize to you. I don't know what to say to excuse myself. In fact, there is nothing for it but to confess that ill health had made me a sleepwalker, and that this is not the first time I have been put into very embarrassing situations by this terribly unfortunate habit."

Mabin frowned frankly. She was an honest, truthful girl, and this man lost her respect the moment he began to tell her what she knew to be falsehoods. Her indignation gave her courage. It was in a much more assured tone that she went on:

"I know it is not the first time, because it happened the very night before. But I know also that you were not asleep, because when you saw that the person in the room was not the person you expected to find there, you went away. Besides, I saw you when you had got out into the garden," added she quickly, "and you were quite wide-awake. At first I thought you must be a burglar, and I was dreadfully frightened; but when I saw you were not, I was more frightened still. And do you think it is right to come into people's houses like that at night and frighten them into fainting fits?"

And Mabin, who had sprung off her chair in her excitement, confronted him with quite an Amazonian air of defiance and reproach.

She felt remorseful, however, almost before she came to the end of her harangue. For he took her onslaught so meekly, so humbly, that she was disarmed. When she had finished, he began to pace quickly up and down the room.

"I know it's wrong, I know it, I know it," he repeated, as if to himself. "I know I ought not to be here at all. I know I am exposing myself and—and others" (his tone dropped into an indescribable softness on the word) "to dangers, to misery, by my presence. And yet I have not the strength of mind to go."

He did not once turn his head to look at his visitor as he uttered these words; indeed she thought, by the monotonous, almost inaudible tones in which he spoke, walking hurriedly up and down, with his eyes on the ground, that he did not even remember that he was not alone. And when he had finished speaking, he still continued his walk up and down, without so much as a glance in her direction, until suddenly, when he had reached the end of the room where she was sitting, he drew himself up and fixing his eyes upon her, asked abruptly:

"Did she know? Did she guess? Did you tell her?"

Mabin had an impulse of amazing astuteness. She had come here to find out why Mr. Banks made burglarious entry into "The Towers!" Here was an opportunity of finding out the relations between him and her friend.

"Tell whom?" said she, pretending not to understand.

"Lady Ma——"

He checked himself at once, and was silent.

"Do you mean Mrs. Dale?" said Mabin.

"Yes, I mean Mrs. Dale," replied he impatiently.

"I didn't tell her anything," said Mabin. "I didn't dare. And she thought she dreamt she saw you the night before; but I know it must have been you she saw."

"She saw me!" cried Mr. Banks, with a sudden eagerness in his voice, a yearning in his eyes, which kept Mabin dumb. Noticing at once the effect his change of manner had on his listener, he checked himself again, and turned his head away.

Still Mabin remained silent. In truth she was beginning to feel alarmed by those glimpses into a story of passion and of sorrow which were being flashed before her innocent young eyes. A blush rose in her cheeks; she got up from her chair, and made a step toward the door, feeling for the first time what a daring thing she had done in making this visit.

"I—I think so. I must suppose so," said she quickly. "And that was why she changed her room."

A look of deepest pain crossed the face of Mr. Banks. His brows contracted, his lips quivered. Mabin, with the righteous indignation of the very young against sins they cannot understand, felt that every blow she struck, cruel though it might be, helped to remove a peril from the path of her friend. With glowing cheeks and downcast eyes she added:

"Why do you try to see her? If you cannot see her openly, why do you try to see her at all? And when only to think she saw you in a dream made her tremble and faint and lock the door."

If she had looked up as she spoke, the words would have died upon her lips. For the agony in his face had become pitiful to see. For a few moments there was dead silence in the room. Although she wanted to go, she felt that she could not leave him like this, and she wanted to know whether her injunctions had had any effect. She was startled by a hollow laugh, and looking up, she met the eyes of Mr. Banks fixed upon her with an expression which seemed to make her suddenly conscious how young and ignorant she was, and how mad to suppose that she could have any influence upon the conduct of older men and women.

"I ought not to have come," she said with a hot blush in her cheeks, "I am too ignorant and too stupid to do anything but harm when I want to do some good to my friends. But please do not laugh at me; I only spoke to you to try to save Mrs. Dale, whom I love, from any more trouble."

"Whom you love! Do you love her too?" said Mr. Banks, with the same change to tenderness which she had noticed in his tone once before. "Well, little one, then you have done your friend some good after all; for I promise you I will not try to see her again."

Mabin was filled with compunction. Mr. Banks did not talk like a wicked man. She longed to put down his unconventional behavior to eccentricity merely; but this was hard, very hard to do. At any rate she had obtained from him a definite promise, and she tried to get another.

"And—please don't think me impertinent—but wouldn't it be better if you went away from here? You know there is always the risk of her seeing you, while you live so near, or of finding out something about you. Please don't think me impertinent; but really, I think, after what I have seen, that if she were to meet you suddenly, and know that she was not dreaming, it would kill her."

Again his face contracted with pain. Mabin, looking down, went on:

"Remember all she has to suffer. When that old woman—an old lady with a hard face—came to see her, and scolded her——"

Mabin stopped. An exclamation on the part of Mr. Banks had made her glance at him; and she was astonished to see, in the hard look of anger which his features had assumed, a likeness, an unmistakable likeness, to the "cat."

"Oh!" cried the girl involuntarily.

"Go on with what you were saying," said Mr. Banks sharply. "An old lady came here, scolded her——"

"And poor Mrs. Dale was miserable. She did not want me to stay with her; she said she was too wicked; she was more miserable than I have ever seen any one before. I am so sorry for her; so sorry."

She stopped. A strange expression, in which there was a gleam of wistful hope, had come into Mr. Banks' face. Mabin put out her hand quickly:

"Good-by," she said. "I think I am glad I came. I'm sure you are not hard-hearted enough to make her any more unhappy than she is."

But Mr. Banks, taking her hand, would not let it go, but walked with her to the door.

"You will let me come with you—as far as the gate of the garden," he said quite humbly. "You are right to trust me. I love your 'Mrs. Dale,' and would not do her any harm. But—it is difficult, very difficult, to know what would be best, happiest, for her."

They were in the hall by this time; and Mr. Banks, still holding the girl's hand very gently in his, had pushed open the door which led into the garden. Instead of going out at once, he turned to look earnestly in Mabin's young fair face.

"I wish you were a little older," he said at last; "then I could tell you the whole story, and you could help me to find out the right thing to do."

"I am nineteen," expostulated Mabin; "and, though he doesn't know it, papa often takes my advice."

Mr. Banks smiled kindly.

"I have no doubt of it," said he. "Nineteen is a great age. But not quite great enough to bear the burden of such a pitiful story. Come."

Reluctantly letting her hand drop, he followed her down the steps into the garden, and Mabin, with all the interest of the visit in her mind, could not repress her delight at finding herself once more in the garden she loved so well. Mr. Banks watched her bright face, as her eyes wandered from the smooth lawn to the borders full of geraniums and pansies, rose-bushes and tall white lilies.

And when she found herself once more in the grass walk, she could not repress an exclamation of pleasure.

"You are fond of your garden," said he. "You must have found it hard to give it up to a stranger!"

Mabin acknowledged the fact with a blush, and, encouraged by his questions, told him some details about her own gardening, and her own pet flowers. Chatting upon such matters as these, they soon reached the side gate in the wall, and passing into the lane, came to the plantation behind "The Towers."

And suddenly to the consternation of Mabin, she heard two voices, within the wood, which she recognized as those of Rudolph and Mrs. Dale.

She turned quickly to Mr. Banks.

He stopped and held out his hand.

"I have not forgotten my promise," said he; "I will leave you now and—and I promise that I will not try to see her again."

The next moment he had disappeared—only just in time. For as the garden gate shut behind him, Mrs. Dale, with a white face and wild eyes, broke through the trees and confronted Mabin.

"Who was that? Whose voice was that?" she asked in almost a shriek.

Mabin sprang forward and put a caressing arm round her.

"He will never come near you again," she whispered, feeling that concealment of the identity of their neighbor with the supposed phantom was no longer possible.

But, to her distress and amazement, Mrs. Dale's face instantly grew rigid with grief and despair, and she sank, trembling and moaning, to the ground.

"I knew it! I was sure of it! Oh, my punishment is too great for me to bear!" she whispered hoarsely.

CHAPTER XII.
A HORRIBLE SECRET.

POOR Mabin gazed down blankly at the crouching figure of Mrs. Dale.

Were the complications of this mysterious history never to end. The little lady had shown terror at the mere sight of this man's portrait; she had abandoned a room in which she had, as she thought, only dreamt of him. And yet now, when Mabin tried to reassure her by repeating his assurance that he would not force himself upon her again, the inconsistent woman gave every sign of the most profound sorrow.

Mabin looked, with her perplexity puckering her pretty face, at Rudolph, who had emerged from the wood in his turn. He however, was too deeply intent upon watching Mrs. Dale to notice his *fiancée's* expression, and Mabin felt a pang of jealousy, which she tried in vain to stifle.

"Don't talk to her," said Rudolph presently, as Mrs. Dale struggling with herself, and still white and trembling, got upon her feet. "Run into the house, Mabin, and get some *eau de Cologne*, and—and don't go too fast, or you will get a headache."

But Mabin, who felt hurt at this evident attempt to get rid of her, lingered, and offered the help of her arm to her friend. But to her astonishment and bitter annoyance, Mrs. Dale not only shrank from her, but cast upon the young girl a look full of resentment.

"Pray, don't take so much trouble. I am quite, quite well," she said coldly. "And I can walk alone, thank you."

She had already withdrawn the arm Mabin had taken, and was plunging into the plantation with reckless steps, as if anxious to bury herself from observation. And she hastily put her handkerchief to her eyes and dashed away the tears which rose as she spoke.

Mabin drew herself up, and choked down a rising sob. What had she done that she should be treated like this? But the climax of her trouble came, when Rudolph, springing across the grass, and keeping his eyes still fixed anxiously on Mrs. Dale, as the little lady in black staggered blindly through the trees, touched her arm gently and whispered:

"You had better leave her for a little while, dear; she will be herself again presently."

Mabin turned her back upon him, and marched off, without a word, in the direction of the house. He called to her to stop, to listen; but she would do neither. Wounded to the core, first by her friend, in whose cause she had been working, and then by her lover, she felt that she could not trust herself in the vicinity of either of them without an outbreak of grief or of anger to which her pride forbade her to give way.

She was in a whirl of feeling; she hardly saw the flowers or the trees as she walked; she scarcely knew whether she trod on grass or on gravel as she made her way straight into the house, shut herself up in her room, and sat down, in a passion of sullen resentment, by one of the high windows.

It seemed to her that she had sat there for hours, sore, perplexed, too miserable to think or to do anything but suffer, when her attention was attracted by a sound which made her start up and look out of the window. There, sauntering along between the broad beds of the kitchen-garden, stooping, from time to time, to hunt under the leaves for a late strawberry, or to gather a flower from the clumps of sweet-william and of clove-pinks which made a fragrant border to the more substantial products of the garden, was Mrs. Dale.

No longer melancholy, no longer silent, but bubbling over with high spirits, and laughing lightly at every other word of her companion, the lady in black looked more radiant than Mabin had ever before seen her, and appeared to be as light-hearted and incapable of serious thought as a child in the sunshine.

And her companion was Rudolph, who followed her, listened to her, laughed with her, and seemed thoroughly satisfied with her society.

This was the cruellest blow of all. That the deceitful woman who could pretend to be so miserable at one moment, and could throw off her grief so lightly the next, should have taken Rudolph and caused him to forget the girl he pretended to care for so much! Mabin watched them with a face wrinkled with despair, until her tears hid them from sight. But even then, Mrs. Dale's voice, always gay, always bright, rang in her ears to the accompaniment of Rudolph's deeper tones.

The girl, however, was not weak-minded enough to cry for long. The sound of the voices had scarcely died away when she sprang to her feet, bathed her face, and did her best to hide the traces of her grief. Pride had come to her assistance. She would show them both that she did not care; that Mrs. Dale might amuse herself with Rudolph, might carry him off altogether if she pleased, and she would not break her heart about it.

She was ready to go downstairs, and was crossing the room for that purpose, when there came a little tap at the door, and Mrs. Dale's voice cried:

"May I come in?"

For answer Mabin turned the handle, and her friend, looking at her inquiringly, tripped into the room with a little affected air of penitence.

"I'm so sorry I was cross, dear, just now. Will you forgive me? I was worried, and unhappy—and—— But I'm better now, and so I've come to ask you to forgive me, and to come down to tea."

She slid her arm round the girl's waist. But Mabin could not disguise the change in her own feelings, which she could not help. She drew herself away with a laugh.

"I'm glad you are happier, and—and better," she said stiffly. "I thought you were, when I saw you just now in the kitchen-garden."

Mrs. Dale looked up at her mischievously.

"Why, you silly child, you have been making yourself miserable. It is of no use for you to try to deny it," said she. "I believe you are jealous, Mabin. You would not be, dear, if you knew all about it."

She spoke very kindly; and by one of those rapid changes of mood and manner which were her greatest charm, her face became suddenly clouded with an expression of gentle sadness.

But Mabin's unhappiness had been too great to be effaced by a few gentle words. And her pride would not allow her to bend, to come to the explanation her friend might be willing to give.

"You are quite wrong," she said coldly; "I am glad to see him so happy. I am not jealous."

And she passed out of the room, as Mrs. Dale invited her to do, and went downstairs with her head very high in the air, and a sense of deep resentment at her heart.

At the dining-room door Rudolph met her, with a rose for her in his hand, and a pretty speech on his lips about her unkindness in hiding herself away for so long. But then, unluckily, Mabin's sharp eyes detected that he threw a glance of intelligence at Mrs. Dale, and choosing instantly to fancy that there was a little conspiracy between the two to "get round" her, she was so reserved and silent and stiff as to make conciliatory advances impossible.

They had tea on the lawn, but it was a very brief affair, for Rudolph jumped up from his seat in about a minute and a half, and said to Mrs. Dale:

"If you will write it out now, I will take it at once."

And then, Mrs. Dale, with a nod of intelligence, rose in her turn, and went quickly into the house.

Mabin sat very still, looking at the grass.

"Let me put your cup down, dear," said Rudolph, who seemed to be subdued by the consciousness of what was in store for him.

As he took the cup, he managed to get hold of her hand.

"And now, Mabin, what's the matter?"

"Nothing," said she with a grand air; "and you are treading on my frock."

"I beg your pardon. I don't think I was treading on your frock, by the bye. It is the table that is on it."

So he went down on one knee, released her dress, and remained in his humble attitude, which brought him too low for her to avoid meeting his eyes, as she would have liked to do.

"And now, Mabin, tell me why you are unkind again so soon."

"You had better get up. Mrs. Dale might see you," was the icy answer.

"Well, and why shouldn't she see me? Mabin, don't behave like this; it isn't worthy of you. I couldn't have thought it possible you would sulk without any cause, as you are doing."

"Without any cause? When Mrs. Dale and you both were unkind, making excuses to send me away, and——"

She stopped, afraid for her self-control. Rudolph taking a seat beside her, went on very quietly:

"She was very unhappy; you had said something, without knowing it, which gave her a great shock. She was hardly mistress of herself; you must have seen that."

"But why was I to be sent away, like a child, without any explanation? When I had just been doing a very difficult thing, too, to try to help her!"

"What was the difficult thing?"

"I had called at 'Stone House,' and seen this man who calls himself Mr. Banks, and got him to promise that he wouldn't get into 'The Towers' at night, as he has done twice, and frighten her."

At this, much to her indignation, Rudolph's mouth curved into an irrepressible smile. Mabin sprang up. But before she had fled very far, he caught her up, and insisted on keeping pace with her, as she ran toward the house.

"Stop, Mabin, and consider. If you run into the house, you will go straight into Mrs. Dale's arms; and if you don't, I will send her to your room after you. You had much better 'have it out' with me."

So she turned and confronted him fiercely.

"Why did you laugh at me?"

"I can hardly tell you. No, don't go off again; I mean that the reason is part of a secret that is not mine."

"A secret, of course; I knew that. A secret which has been confided to you, but which I am not to know."

Rudolph was silent.

"Can you expect me to be satisfied, to be laughed at and neglected, while you and Mrs. Dale exchange confidences, and forg-g-get me?"

"Now, Mabin, you are silly, my darling, silly, childish! You have known just as well as I that there was a secret somewhere. Can't you be content to wait till the proper time comes for you to be told, instead of behaving like an inquisitive school-girl?"

Now this was the very worst sort of speech he could have made. If Rudolph had not been himself a good deal excited that afternoon by the story which Mrs. Dale had confided to his ears, he would have exercised greater restraint, greater choice in his words, and would have given more consideration to his *fiancée's* point of view.

Mabin grew white.

"I can wait, certainly," she said with a sudden change to an extremely quiet manner and tone, "for the great secret which absorbed you so deeply. But there is another, a little mystery, which I want to know now; and that is—how a woman who is in the depths of despair at four o'clock, as Mrs. Dale appeared to be, can be in the very highest spirits at five? Or is that a secret I have to wait to know?"

"It's all part of the same story," replied Rudolph humbly, feeling perhaps that greater demands were being made upon her patience than was quite fair. "And I can only repeat that you will know everything presently."

"And why not now?"

"The whole thing was confided to me, and I don't feel at liberty to say any more even to you! Surely you can trust me, can trust us both. Why, Mabin, I thought you were so proud of your loyalty to your friends!"

The tears sprang to the girl's eyes. She was giving way, and yet feeling all the time that she had not been well treated, when unluckily she noticed a little movement on the part of her companion, and looked up quickly enough to see that Mrs. Dale, with a mischievous smile on her face, was standing at the door of the house, and waving a strip of paper to him as a signal.

"Go. Make haste. Mrs. Dale wants you!" cried Mabin bitterly.

And without leaving him time to protest or explain, she ran away.

That evening passed uncomfortably for both Mabin and Mrs. Dale. When they met at dinner, they both showed traces of recent tears on their pretty faces, and both unwisely tried to behave as if nothing had happened to disturb the usual course of things.

Mrs. Dale did indeed make advances toward a modified half-confidence; but it was so abundantly evident that she did so against her will, and that she was afraid of saying too much, that she repelled rather than encouraged the shy, proud girl.

Rudolph did not return. This was another sore point with poor Mabin, who ended by persuading herself that Mrs. Dale had succeeded in alienating from her the affections of her lover.

So that the hours dragged wearily by until bed-time, and both ladies showed an unusual anxiety to get early to bed.

But next morning there was a change in Mrs. Dale's manner; she had lost her feverish high spirits, and was in such a state of nervous irritability that even the sound of Mabin's voice, coldly asking a question at the breakfast-table, made her start and flush painfully. Her eyes were heavy; her cheeks were white; there were dark lines under her eyes which told of a sleepless night.

Mabin felt sorry for her, and was quite ready to "kiss and be friends." After all, she said to herself with resignation not unmingled with bitterness, if Rudolph found the lovely widow with the interesting history more attractive than a girl with no fascinating mystery attached to her, it was not his fault, and it was not surprising. She felt ashamed now of her jealousy and ill-temper of the previous evening, excusable as they had been. And she deliberately made up her mind that, whatever happened, she would take matters quietly; and even if Rudolph deserted her altogether for Mrs. Dale, that she would give him up without a murmur, whatever the effort cost her.

After all, what was the use, she said to herself with a heavy sigh, of trying to keep a man's love against his will? It had been a very fleeting happiness, that of his love; but the superstitious feeling the girl had had about its suddenness made her inclined to accept the loss of it as inevitable; and no one would have guessed, from her calm manner and measured voice, that Mabin was suffering the keenest sorrow she had ever known.

It was Mrs. Dale who was reticent to-day. She told Mabin that she expected a visitor that evening, but she did not say who it was. And from the fever which burned in her eyes, and the restlessness which increased upon her as the day went on, the young girl guessed that some matter of great importance was to be discussed or arranged.

Was the visitor to be Mr. Banks? she asked herself. But she did not dare to put the question to her hostess.

One unprecedented occurrence signalized the occasion. The musty drawing-room was turned out, aired, and prepared for the reception of the visitor.

"Do take your work in there, and leave it about, and try to make the place look a little less like a charnel-house," cried Mrs. Dale to Mabin that afternoon, when they had gone together to inspect the state apartment.

"It does look rather dreary certainly," admitted Mabin. "But it won't look so bad to any one who hasn't been used, like us, to knowing it is always shut up."

"That's true. I hadn't thought of that. However, I still beg you to drop a few bits of filoselle about, and to read a few books and strew them about.

And I'll run out and get some bits of copper beech and bracken to fill those yawning bowls. Flowers would be quite lost in them."

"Not the peonies. They would look splendid!" Mabin called out after her, as the widow went out through the French window on to the gravel path outside.

It was already late in the afternoon, and, darkened as it was by the trees and shrubs which grew near the large windows, the room was so dimly lighted that Mabin took her work—it was still the cooking apron—to the window. It had required some self-control to take up a piece of work to which such recent memories were attached; and as she sewed, Mabin had great difficulty in keeping back the tears. Here were the very stitches Rudolph had put in, the very bag on which their fingers had closed together. She felt the thrill of that contact now.

And even as she let the apron fall into her lap, while the longing to hear his voice speak tender words in her ear stirred in her heart and made it beat fast, she heard his footstep on the gravel outside; she saw him pass the window.

Scarcely repressing the cry: "Rudolph! Rudolph!" which rose to her lips, she saw that he was hurrying across the grass without having seen her. And looking out of the window, she saw that Mrs. Dale was standing under the lime trees, holding out her hand to him with a smile of greeting.

And the look of confidence and pleasure which irradiated the widow's face filled Mabin with despair.

She stood still at the window, but she no longer saw anything; she was blinded by her tears. She hardly heard the door of the drawing-room open, or, if she heard, she did not notice it. She did not turn her head when the door closed.

It was not until a hard voice, close to her, said dryly:

"Are you the young lady whom I met here before—who refused to take the warning I gave?" that Mabin, dashing away the tears from her blinded eyes, recognized in the erect figure standing beside her Mrs. Dale's former mysterious visitor.

"I—I beg your pardon," said Mabin hastily; "I—I did not see you come in. You want to see Mrs. Dale. I will go and tell her."

"You need not take that trouble," replied the majestic lady in the same hard tones as before. "She expects me. She sent for me by telegraph yesterday." And following the glance Mabin threw across the lawn, she asked quickly, and in a harsher tone than ever: "Who is the young man with her?"

"Mr. Bonnington, the Vicar's son," answered Mabin in a low voice.

"And what is he doing here?"

"He's a friend of Mrs. Dale's, and a friend of mine too," added the girl with the generous wish to save her friend from the anger she saw in the elder woman's eyes. "I am engaged to him."

"Engaged to him! Engaged to marry him!" repeated the other sharply. "And you trust him with that woman!"

Mabin's loyalty was fired by the tone.

"Yes. She is my friend," said she proudly.

The elder lady uttered a short, hard sound, which she meant for a derisive laugh.

"Well, you are an independent young person, upon whom warnings are thrown away. However, it may be of passing interest for you to know that the lady you call your friend—" Mabin put her hands to her ears, instinctively guessing that she was to hear some horrible thing. In the darkness of the room the face above her seemed to her to be distorted with the passion of a fiend as, in a voice so piercing that the girl heard it distinctly, in spite of herself; she went on: "that the lady you call your friend has ruined the life of a man who loved her." And Mabin caught her breath, thinking of the white face of Mr. Banks. Still the hard voice went inexorably on: "and that she murdered her own husband!"

Mabin uttered a shriek, as her hands fell down from her ears.

CHAPTER XIII.
MRS. DALE'S VERSION OF THE STORY.

THE terrible words rang in Mabin's ears as she remained staring at the hard, vindictive face of the elder woman, hardly yet realizing all that the accusation meant.

Mrs. Dale had murdered her own husband! Surely, surely it was not true. She might be vain, frivolous, a coquette; but a murderess! The girl instinctively shook her head.

The gaunt visitor, with an acid and unpleasant smile, sat down on one of the fragile-looking *papier-maché* chairs, with mother-of-pearl inlaid ornamentation, which dated the furnishing of the room.

"I—I can't believe it. No, I won't believe it!" whispered Mabin hoarsely.

"There is no necessity for your doing so," retorted the other with indifference. "As it is a very unpleasant thing to believe, indeed, I think you are wise to discredit it. And since she has alienated all her old friends, it is fortunate that she can manage to find new ones."

As the lady spoke, Mabin felt the horror she had experienced melt gradually into pity for the poor little lady whom this hard woman had in her power. And with compassion came resistance.

"Why shouldn't she have friends?" she asked hotly. "Mrs. Dale is not a hypocrite. She is deeply sorry for what wrong she has done; she never denies that she has done something which has spoiled her life. And I like her better for being able to be happy in spite of it, sometimes, than if she pretended she could never smile again."

"Well, of course, for such a trifle as the murder of her husband, you could not expect a woman of her light temperament to trouble herself very long!" said the visitor with grim irony.

"I don't mean that. I know how much she suffers. But look how young she is. How could you expect that she could never be happy for a single moment any more? Doesn't God forgive us our sins, when we repent truly? And isn't it by His laws that we can't be numb to any feeling but one all our lives?"

"You are a very powerful advocate, I am sure! Perhaps if you had had a son whose life had been ruined by this woman's conduct, you would be less enthusiastic."

These words startled Mabin, and made her look at the harsh visitor in a new light. And she saw, or fancied she saw, in the handsome but stern features of the old lady, a trace of the worn face of her father's tenant. She came a step closer, with her eyes intently fixed on the lady's countenance.

"Are you," she asked in a whisper, "a relation of Mr. Banks?"

The visitor started, and seemed intensely astonished, and even alarmed, by this question. She made no answer for a few moments, which she passed in deep thought. Then, raising her head, and looking straight into the girl's eyes, she said calmly:

"And who is Mr. Banks?"

"One of the *old* friends of Mrs. Dale, who cares for her as much as any new one!" replied Mabin promptly.

The other lady frowned.

"I didn't want an epigram. I wanted to know who this Mr. Banks was, and where you had met him," she said tartly.

Mabin, seeing what a strong impression her rash words had made wished she had not uttered them. While she was still wondering how she should get out of her difficulty, with as little harm as possible to Mrs. Dale, a sharply uttered question made her start.

"Has he—has this Mr. Banks met M-M-Mrs. Dale?"

She stammered over the lady's name, just as Mr. Banks himself had done.

"No," answered Mabin promptly.

And at this answer the old lady, suddenly breaking down in the intensity of her relief, fell back in her chair and gasped out:

"Thank Heaven!"

Mabin's thoughts moved quickly. Stirred by the excitement of this interview, she tried to find a way of serving Mrs. Dale; and it occurred to her if this fierce old lady could meet Mr. Banks, he would perhaps be able to tone down her ferocity. After a short pause she asked:

"Would you like to see him?"

"What? Is he here? You told me——"

The old lady was now so much excited and alarmed that she could scarcely gasp out the words.

"He is staying not far from here," replied Mabin cautiously.

The visitor got up.

"No, I do not wish to see him. I wish to see no one but Mrs. Dale. I cannot understand why she keeps me waiting like this. I have come all the way from Yorkshire to oblige her, at great inconvenience to myself."

Mabin could not understand it either, knowing as she did that Mrs. Dale had expected her visitor. In the present state of affairs every unlooked-for occurrence assumed a portentous aspect, so that she felt rather alarmed.

"I will go and tell her you are here," she said.

She was glad to be out of the presence of this terrible woman. And as she ran out into the garden and then dropped into a sedate walk as she passed the drawing-room windows, her heart went out to the old lady's victim more than it did to that of the young one.

Under the lime-trees, where she had last seen Mrs. Dale, she met Rudolph alone. She greeted him with a white face, and without a smile.

"Where is she—Mrs. Dale?" she then asked at once.

Rudolph, flushing a little at her manner, answered gravely:

"She was sent for to see some one, and went indoors. But then she fainted, and they took her into the dining-room."

"Thank you. I must go to her."

Rudolph ran after her as she returned to the house.

"What has happened? You have learned something, found out something. What is it?"

Mabin turned, and he saw that the tears were springing to her eyes.

"I have, oh, I have!" she whispered hoarsely. "But don't ask me now. I can't tell you now. I must go to her."

He did not detain her, and she ran into the house and softly opened the door of the dining-room. Mrs. Dale was lying on the hard horsehair sofa, with her eyes closed. Two of the servants were present, with fans and smelling-salts, and the usual remedies for a fainting-fit.

As usual in the case of a household where there is a skeleton in the cupboard, the servants took sides, and each of the opposing parties was represented on this occasion. For while the housemaid, Annie, was her mistress' sworn champion, the parlormaid, who also waited on Mrs. Dale, was suspected to be in the pay of the enemy, the old lady now in the drawing-room.

As Mabin entered Mrs. Dale opened her eyes, and sat up.

"I must go, I must go," she said in a weak and husky voice, as if hardly yet mistress of herself.

"Yes, you shall go, in one minute," said Mabin. And springing forward with ready kindness and affection in her face, she signed to the servants to leave them together. "Let me do your hair for you; I can do it, I know I can," she went on gently, touching the beautiful fair hair which had become loose and disordered, and looking with tender compassion into the blue eyes, which seemed to have lost their brilliancy, their bright color.

Mrs. Dale stared with wide-open, dull eyes at the forms of the two servants, as they left the room. Then she turned her head slowly, and looked long at the young girl whose arm was now around her.

"Why are you so kind to me now?" she asked at last in a weak and almost childish voice that went straight to Mabin's heart. "You were not kind last night!"

The first answer Mabin gave was a slight pressure of the arm upon Mrs. Dale's shoulder. Then Mabin bent down and whispered in her ear:

"I didn't know so much then!"

The little slender form in her arm shivered.

"What—what do you know now?" Then recollecting the events which had preceded her own loss of consciousness, she suddenly sprang off the sofa. "I know! I know! That cruel woman told you! I must go to her; oh, I must go!"

"Well, let me do up your dress first."

And Mrs. Dale then perceived that the upper part of her bodice had been unfastened by the maids, and that her face was still wet from the sprinkling of water they had given her. She submitted to Mabin's assistance, therefore, in arranging her hair and her dress, without another word being exchanged between them. When she was ready to go, however, she stopped on her way to the door, and gave Mabin one long, curious look. It made the girl spring forward, with a world of sympathy in her eyes.

"Oh, I'm so sorry for you!" she whispered. "So very, very sorry. Much more than before I knew anything."

Then Mrs. Dale gave way, and seeming for the first time to recover her powers of thought and of speech, she sank down on the nearest chair, and burst into tears, natural, healing tears, while she poured into Mabin's ears a broken, incoherent confession:

"It is quite true that I did it—did what she told you. But you know, oh, Mabin, you do know how bitterly I have repented it! I would have given my life to have been able to live those few minutes over again! What did she tell you? Tell me, tell me! And how did she say it? Of course she made the very worst of it; but it was bad enough without that. Oh, Mabin, Mabin! Don't you think she might forgive me now?"

While she talked in this wandering and excited way Mabin hardly knew what to do; whether to try to divert her thoughts, or to let her know in what a vixenish and hard manner the elder woman had made the announcement of the terrible action which had cut short one life and ruined another.

"Of course she ought to forgive you!" she said at last. "But you must not give way to despair if she does not. She is a hard woman; she will never treat you as tenderly as your own friends do."

She paused, not liking to tell Mrs. Dale that the visitor was waiting for her, and wondering whether her friend had forgotten the fact. As she glanced toward the door, Mrs. Dale caught her eye, and suddenly threw herself upon her knees, burying her head in the girl's lap.

"Oh, I daren't, I daren't go in—just yet!" she whispered almost pleadingly. "I know I sent for her; I know I must see her; but now that the moment has come, I feel as if I could not bear it. I know how she will look—what she will say. And it is upon her, all upon her, that my life, my very life depends!"

Mabin said nothing. She could not help thinking, from the wild words and wilder manner of the wretched woman before her, that the great strain of her crime and her repentance had ended by weakening her mind. Unless——

The girl drew a long breath, frightened by the awful possibility, which had just occurred to her, that the grim visitor in the drawing-room had been threatening Mrs. Dale with the extreme penalty of her crime. Mrs. Dale's words—"My life depends upon her!" were explicit enough. Instinctively Mabin's arm closed more tightly round the sobbing woman.

"Hush, hush, dear!" she whispered soothingly. "She will not dare, she will not dare to be more cruel than she has been already! You must try and be brave, and to bear her hard words; but she won't do anything more than scold you!"

In the midst of her grief Mrs. Dale looked up in the girl's face with a sad smile.

"Oh, she has dared so much more than that already!" she said hopelessly. "I don't want to excuse myself—nothing can excuse me—but I want you to know the share she had in it all. For she had a share. It would never have happened but for her."

Mrs. Dale sprang to her feet, and walking up and down the room with her little white hands clinched till the nails marked her flesh, she began to pour into the young girl's ears a story which kept her hearer fascinated, spellbound.

"Listen, listen!" said Mrs. Dale in a low, breathless voice, without glancing at the girl. "It is not a story for you; I would never have told you a word of it if it had not been forced upon us both. But now, as you have heard so much, told in one way, you must hear the rest, told in another."

Mabin said nothing.

In fact, it seemed to her that Mrs. Dale hardly cared whether she listened or not. She went on with her story in the same hurried, monotonous tone, as if it was merely the relief of putting it into words that she wanted:

"I had always been spoiled, always had my own way, until I was married. My father and mother both died when I was a little thing of six, and I lived with my guardian and his family, and they let me do just as I liked. I was supposed to be rich, almost an heiress; but when my guardian died, it was found that the money had all gone; I had nothing. I was not yet eighteen then. And Sir Geoffrey Mallyan wanted to marry me. Every one said I must; that there was nothing else for me to do. I didn't care for him; but then I didn't care for any one else; so nobody thought it mattered. It was taken for granted, don't you see, that there was no question of my saying no."

Mrs. Dale stopped short, and for the first time looked at Mabin:

"That's what people always think, that it doesn't matter whom a girl marries, if she's very young. But it does, oh, it does! And he had a brother——"

Mabin started, and thought at once of Mr. Banks.

"A younger brother, who had been ordered home from India on sick leave. No, I didn't care for him," she went on emphatically, reading the expression of sympathy on the girl's face. "But he was livelier than his grave brother, my husband, and we were very good friends. Nobody would have thought that there was any harm in that if old Lady Mallyan hadn't interfered. You can guess now, I suppose, who Lady Mallyan is!"

Mabin nodded emphatically without speaking.

"She came posting to the place to find out the evil which was only in her own mind. We had been getting on quite well together, my husband and I. I was rather afraid of him, but I liked him, and he was kind to me. I believe he was really fond of me; and that I should have grown fond of him. I was fond of him in a way; but he was fifteen years older than I, and very quiet and grave in his manners. But he let me do what I liked, and took me to all the dances and races I wanted, and was proud of me, and seemed pleased that I should enjoy myself. But when his mother came, everything was changed. She had great influence with him, and she told him that he was spoiling me, and making me fit for nothing but amusement, and that these constant gayeties were ruining my character. And so he told me, very gently, very kindly, that I must settle down, and live a quieter life.

"I was sorry, disappointed, and not too grateful to Lady Mallyan. Would you have been? Would anybody have been? But I submitted. There were some scenes first, of course. I had been spoiled; I am bad-tempered, I know; and I was indignant with her for her interference. What harm had I been doing, after all? I was not unhappy, however, and it was easy to reconcile myself to everything but to her. For she seemed to have settled down in my husband's house, and I did not dare to hint that I resented this. Then things went on smoothly for a time. I had given up my balls, and nearly all what my mother-in-law was pleased to call 'dissipations.' But now that I was oftener at home, I naturally saw more of Willie, my husband's brother, than before, since he was not strong enough to go out so much as Sir Geoffrey and I had done.

"We were all very anxious about him, as he seemed to be on the verge of consumption. He was very bright and amusing, however, even then, and I was certainly more at ease with him than I was with my mother-in-law, or even with my own husband, who was a silent and undemonstrative man. But it was shameful of Lady Mallyan to suspect that I cared more for him than for my husband; it never entered into his head or mine to suppose any one would think such a wicked thing; and certainly Sir Geoffrey would never have thought of such a thing except at the suggestion of his mother.

"I cannot tell you, child, of the wretchedness this miserable old woman brought about, in her jealousy at Sir Geoffrey's love for me, and her anxiety to get back the influence over him which she thought I had usurped. Of course if I had been an older woman, as old as I am now, for example, I should have rebelled; I should have insisted on her leaving the house where she had brought nothing but misery. I should have known how to take my proper place as mistress of the house in which she was only an interloper.

"But I did not know how to do it, although I knew what I ought to do.

"So it went on, the misery of every one growing greater every day, Willie and I feeling a restraint which made us afraid to exchange a word under her eyes; my husband growing shorter in his manner, more reserved in his speech, having had his mind poisoned against his brother and against me.

"At last a crisis came. Willie told us that he was going away. I knew he was in no fit state to travel, but I did not dare to tell him to stay, or to tell the fears I felt for him. When he was ready to go, I spoke out to him at last. We were in the drawing-room, standing by the fire, and I told him it was his mother who had made us all miserable and afraid to speak to one another, and I begged him to come with me to Sir Geoffrey, and to back me up in telling him the truth, in insisting that Lady Mallyan should leave the house.

"'If you go away now, without speaking to Geoffrey,' I said, 'I shall be left in the power of this hateful, wicked woman for the rest of my life. For she will never leave of her own accord; and I dare not speak to Geoffrey about her with no one to back me up.'

"And then I saw Lady Mallyan's shadow outside the window on the path. She had been listening, she was always listening; hoping to find out something as we said good-by.

"I ran to the window, but she escaped me. When Willie was gone, I went to look for my husband. He was in the gun-room, looking harder than usual. His mother had just left him. I had never seen him look so stern, and I was frightened. I began to see that I was powerless against the mischievous woman who was spoiling our lives.

"'Geoffrey!' I said. 'What has your mother been saying to you? She has been saying something unkind I know; something untrue, probably. What is it?'

"Then he said something which made me feel as if I had been turned into stone. Lady Mallyan had been with him, had misrepresented my words to Willie, had put a hideous meaning into all we had said. I forget Sir Geoffrey's exact words; if I remembered them I would not repeat them. But they were cold, full of suspicion. They roused in me a mad feeling of hatred. I can remember that I shook till my dress rustled; that I could not speak. Then—God forgive me! I took up a little pistol—revolver—I don't know what they call it; but it was something so small it looked like a toy—and, hardly knowing what I did, I pointed it at him, and—and—he cried out, and fell down.

"I don't know what happened then, whether I shrieked out, or what happened. But they came in, a lot of them, and took me away. And—and I never saw him again. She would not even let me see him when he lay dead. Though I begged, how I begged!"

Suddenly Mrs. Dale stopped in her speech, and crossed quickly to the door. Flinging it open suddenly, she revealed Lady Mallyan, standing within a couple of feet of it, erect, very pale.

Mrs. Dale smiled.

"Come in, pray come in, your ladyship. You have not lost your old habits, I see," she said with cutting emphasis as she bowed to her visitor.

CHAPTER XIV.
NO MERCY.

IT was with a throbbing brain and a heavy heart that Mabin, dismissed by Mrs. Dale with a warm pressure of the hand and a little pathetic smile, went through the hall and out of the house.

What was the meaning of old Lady Mallyan's coming? Why had Mrs. Dale sent for her? Surely, the girl felt, there could be but one answer to this question; and in that answer lay the key to the mystery about "Mr. Banks."

Mabin remembered the likeness she had seen in his face, in one of his sterner moments, to the visitor whom she now knew as Lady Mallyan. And she could have little doubt, on putting together the facts of the story she had just heard and the details she knew concerning her father's tenant, that it was indeed Sir Geoffrey Mallyan's brother Willie, one of the causes, if not the sole cause, of the tragedy which had wrecked Mrs. Dale's life, who had settled down, unknown to the lady herself, as her nearest neighbor.

A hot blush came into Mabin's face, alone though she was, as this conclusion forced itself upon her. For even she, young and innocent as she was, could not help seeing that his behavior, since he had lived at Stone House, was inconsistent with Mrs. Dale's account of the blameless relations which had existed between them.

Mrs. Dale had represented this "Willie" as a light-hearted young fellow, who had felt only the comradeship of a younger brother toward his brother's beautiful wife. But "Mr. Banks" had behaved, not only like a lover, but like a lover, once favored, whom despair had driven to the verge of madness.

On the other hand, Mabin, in her loyalty toward her friend, was ready to believe that, even if the feelings these two unhappy creatures had had for each other had been less innocent than Mrs. Dale had represented, they had been themselves less to blame than either of the two other persons concerned in the terrible history.

Mrs. Dale, naturally enough constrained by her own remorse to speak well of her dead husband, had yet been able to give no very attractive picture of the man who had misunderstood his young wife, frightened away her confidence, and allowed himself to be alienated from her by the interference of his mother. And of that mother herself Mabin had seen enough to be more than ready to give her her fair share of the blame.

The young girl's heart went out, more than it had ever done before, to the little woman, whom nature had made so frivolous, and circumstances so miserable, and around whom misfortune seemed to be closing once more.

It was the one gleam of comfort she had to know how sincerely Mrs. Dale was trying to do what was right in the matter. Instead of attempting to see "Mr. Banks," which would have been easy enough for her to do, she had sent for his mother, repugnant though such a course must always be to her; so that, whatever indiscretion she might have shown in the past, it was clear that she meant to keep herself free from all suspicion now.

And this was the more creditable on her part, so Mabin felt, since the strange elation she had shown by fits and starts since the day before, when she heard the voice of "Mr. Banks" for the first time, proved clearly that she was not so indifferent, not so unimpressionable, as she had professed to be.

And here Mabin felt her heart grow very tender; she pictured to herself what she would feel, if circumstances were to put Rudolph and herself in the same position toward each other, as were "Mr. Banks" and "Mrs. Dale."

If she were to have to live within a stone's throw of him, not only always loving, always longing, but conscious that the same feelings which drew her heart toward him were forever drawing him toward her.

Mabin began to cry softly. And then the application of the story to her own case caused her thoughts to take another turn; and she asked herself, with the generous Quixotism of her youth and her loyal nature, whether she ought not to wish for, to encourage, the process by which Rudolph's love was being diverted from herself, the uninteresting, awkward girl without any history, to the unhappy lady around whom there clung the romance of a tragedy.

These questions, which had indeed risen in her mind before, but which had now acquired a new force with her extended knowledge, were entirely consistent with the bent of Mabin's mind. Accustomed from her childhood to consider others rather than herself, and inclined by her own modesty to underrate her deserts as well as her attractions, she found it easy, not indeed to stifle her own feelings, but to control them. She told herself that she would show Rudolph no more petulance, no more "childish" jealousy or curiosity; and if, as seemed inevitable, he found that he had made a mistake in thinking he cared for herself, she would be the first to wish him happiness with a more attractive bride.

Perhaps it showed rather a touching sense of her own devotion to her lover, that Mabin never once doubted his power to console Mrs. Dale for all her troubles, nor that lady's readiness to be comforted by him.

And it was while these thoughts were fresh in her mind that Mabin, turning the angle in the path toward the kitchen-garden, came face to face with Rudolph.

Meeting him at such a moment, it was not surprising that she stopped short, turned first red, then white, and presented to his view a countenance so deeply impressed with a sort of shy alarm, that the young man was rather puzzled as to the kind of greeting he might expect.

Recovering herself quickly, Mabin wisely put off explanations by dashing straight into an exciting subject:

"Oh, do you know," she asked in a hurried, constrained voice, "that I have had to leave poor Mrs. Dale to that dragon? Oh yes, I know who she is now; I know who they both are. Mrs. Dale herself has told me that, told me everything;" added Mabin, in answer to an interrogative and puzzled look which she detected on his face.

Rudolph looked dubious.

"Everything?" he repeated doubtfully.

"And," went on Mabin with calm triumph, "old Lady Mallyan has told me something too. And as I had a long talk with Mr. Banks yesterday, I think perhaps the tables are turned, and I know more than you do now."

Mabin seated herself, as she spoke, on the garden seat which was placed, most charmingly as far as picturesque effect was concerned, but most inconveniently, if one considered earwigs and green flies, under a tall lime-tree and against a dark hedge of yew. Rudolph was intensely relieved to find that her jealous and angry mood of the evening before had passed away; and although he was puzzled by her new manner, which was easy, friendly, but not affectionate, he thought it better to fall in with her mood and not to risk the pleasure of the moment, by asking for explanations just yet. Mabin, on her side, felt a curiously pleasant sense of present enjoyment and irresponsibility. It was happiness to be with Rudolph, without any dispute to trouble their intercourse. And she found that by turning his attention and her own away from themselves to the subject of Mrs. Dale and her troubles, she got not only the full delight of Rudolph's attention, but the satisfaction that she was stifling, if not conquering, her own weakness.

Rudolph was charmed by the new and undefinable change to greater frankness, to less shyness, in her manner.

"Well," said he, pulling down the bough of a guelder rose-tree and beginning with great precision to strip off the leaves, "I couldn't help myself, could I? I couldn't tell you somebody else's secrets without permission. And you see you haven't had to wait very long to know all about it."

"Oh, I'm not thinking about that," said Mabin superbly. "It was annoying at the time not to know what you were all talking about; but I soon got over that. What I am thinking about now is the best thing to be done for Mrs. Dale. You know who this Mr. Banks is, I suppose?"

Her assumption of a lofty standpoint of deep knowledge combined with great indifference amused Rudolph.

"Do you?" retorted he.

"I suppose," she answered almost in a whisper, and looking down on the ground as she spoke, "that he is Lady Mallyan's son Willie."

Rudolph looked astonished.

"You do know something then!" said he at last. "Yes, I suppose he is."

"And Mrs. Dale knows it?—knew it yesterday, I suppose?—when she heard his voice?"

"Yes, I think so, I suppose so. But I must tell you that she was so much upset that I didn't attempt to ask her any questions about it. I only tried to quiet her, and offer, when she said she must see Lady Mallyan, to send off the telegram."

Mabin, too much excited to sit still, sprang to her feet on the gravel path beside him.

"Isn't it hard? Oh, isn't it hard for her? She does exactly what is right, what is best. She ought not to be persecuted by either of them, by mother or son!"

But instead of answering her fervent outbreak in the same tone, or at least with sympathy, she saw, to her indignation, that Rudolph had difficulty in suppressing a smile.

"The persecution won't last long," said he. Then noting the revulsion of feeling expressed in Mabin's face, he added quickly: "When Lady Mallyan and Mr. Banks meet, they will have to come to an understanding; and I can answer for it that after that Mrs. Dale will be left in peace."

"That's what Mr. Banks himself seems to think," said Mabin ingenuously. "But Lady Mallyan was shocked when she heard he lived so near, and she doesn't want to meet him."

Rudolph was in an instant on fire with excitement.

"Oh, doesn't she, though? Then I'll take jolly good care that she shall!" He took three or four rapid steps away from her and came back again. His face was glowing with excitement. "Look here, Mabin, I want you to mount guard over the house, and see that the old lady doesn't get away before I get back with Mr. Banks. Mind, it is very important. You must do anything rather than let her go. It's just possible she may get an idea of something of the kind, and may try to get away."

"All right," said Mabin very quietly, but none the less showing in the firm set of her lips and the steadiness of her eyes that she would prove a firm ally. "But don't be long gone; for I am afraid of what may be going on between that hard woman and poor little Mrs. Dale!"

"I'll be as quick as I can. You may trust me."

And then, taking her entirely by surprise, he flung his arms round her, pressed upon her startled lips a long kiss, and ran off before she had breath to utter a word.

She had just sense enough left to remember her promise, to stagger round to the front of the house, and to take her place as sentinel under the dining-room wall. There was no window on this side, the space where one had originally been having been blocked up and filled with a painted imitation of one. It was impossible therefore for Mabin to tell, in this position, whether the interview between the two ladies was over or not.

So she went into the hall, where it was now so dark that she felt her way, stumbling, in the direction of the dining-room door. She was close to it before she was assured, so low was the voice speaking within the room, that the ladies were still there. But the piteous, subdued tones of Mrs. Dale, which met her ear as she came near, told her that the little lady in black was still pleading to her tyrant.

Withdrawing quickly, her heart throbbing in sympathy with the unfortunate woman, Mabin returned to the garden, and waited near the garden gate.

She now had leisure to dwell on that intoxicating kiss, which had for the moment thrown her back into the world of happiness into which Rudolph's avowal of love had introduced her, and from which more recent events had seemed to combine to thrust her out. Could it be that he was still the same as ever, in spite of her jealous fears, of her Quixotic imaginings? Mabin's brain seemed to be set on fire at the thought. She began to look out at the treeless fields which lay between "The Towers" and the sea, with eyes which saw nothing. Though mechanically from time to time she turned to glance at the front door of the house, she had forgotten for whom she was watching.

Suddenly she was startled by the sound of light footsteps on the gravel behind her, and looking round, she saw the parlormaid running toward the gate.

"The cab, miss, have you seen the cab? The lady wants to go now, and of course the stupid man is out of sight."

"It is at the corner of the road," answered Mabin, waking up to the realities of life with a start. "But don't go for it yet. Mr. Bonnington wants to speak to Lady Mallyan first."

The girl was evidently startled and impressed by the discovery that Mabin knew the visitor's name. She hesitated.

"But she wants to catch a train, miss!" she protested at last.

As Mabin was about to answer, a figure in the road outside caught her eye. The maid saw it too.

"Who—who was that?" Mabin asked quickly.

The maid, who looked rather scared, hesitated, stammered.

"Was it—Mrs. Dale?" pursued Mabin almost in a whisper.

And as she spoke, her heart sickened with a vague fear. Quickly as the form had passed by, and disappeared from sight in the deep shadows of the trees at the bend of the road below, there had been something about its rapid and noiseless flight, in the very bend of the head and flutter of the dress, which alarmed the young girl.

Besides if it was Mrs. Dale, what was she doing, at this late hour of the evening, on the road which led down to the cliff, to the sea? She must have gone out by the door at the back of the house, too;—surely a strange thing to do!

But even as these thoughts crowded into her mind, there came another and less disquieting one. The road she had taken passed the front of "Stone House;" perhaps she had gone to seek herself an interview with "Mr. Banks."

Even as she made this suggestion to herself, and while the voice of the maid still murmured that she must go and fetch the cab, Mabin heard men's voices in the road below.

Recognizing that of Rudolph, she stepped outside the gates, and waited with anxiety for his appearance.

But he came slowly; perhaps, thought Mabin, he was talking to Mrs. Dale. She listened more intently; but as the voices came gradually nearer, she was able to assure herself that they were only those of Rudolph and of "Mr. Banks." Scarcely able to control her anxiety, she stepped out through the gates into the road, at the very moment that Lady Mallyan's harsh voice sounded behind her, speaking to the parlormaid:

"Where is my cab?"

Rudolph heard these words, and he hurried forward with his companion. It was now almost dark. Mabin saw who the man was beside him, but she could not distinguish his face.

"I beg your pardon, madam," said Rudolph, raising his hat and walking quickly after the old lady, who had passed through the gate and was hurrying down the road: "Your son wishes to speak to you. He cannot walk so fast as you, but he has sent me with this message."

She stopped short, appeared to hesitate, and then turned back without a word.

It was close to where Mabin stood, stupidly, not knowing exactly what was going to happen, or what she ought to do on behalf of Mrs. Dale, that mother and son met.

Dark as it was out there, with only a line of pale yellow light left in the horizon, shading off through sea-green into the blue above, Mabin saw enough to know that the meeting was one of deep import. Old Lady Mallyan seemed uneasy; the harshness which Mabin had hitherto believed to be her most salient quality had almost disappeared from her tones as she addressed her son:

"I am sorry," she said, quite gently, as she put out her arms toward him, "to find you here. It can do no good. It might have done great harm. Why did you not let me know where you were? Why did you deceive me?"

But "Mr. Banks" did not accept the offered caress of the outstretched arms.

"I will tell you why, mother, presently. But now, where is Dorothy? I want to see her. I must see her. Surely," he went on as she did not at first answer, "surely she will see me now you are here. Surely she will not refuse!"

There was again a silence of a few seconds, during which Mabin, who had only withdrawn a little way, and who was striving to attract the attention of Rudolph, who stood with his back to her, uttered a little cry of pain and distress.

Mr. Banks went on impatiently:

"Where is she? Is she in the house? I must go to her; I must see her!"

Then Lady Mallyan spoke, in a voice which was greatly changed. She seemed to be trying to control some real alarm.

"You cannot," she said quickly. "She will not see you. She refuses—absolutely. As a gentleman you cannot persist. She is as hard and cold-hearted as ever. She will not see you again. She has gone away."

At these words, which Mabin heard, the young girl uttered a sharp cry. But "Mr. Banks" did not heed her. He spoke again, in such piteous tones that Mabin and Rudolph, young and susceptible both, felt their hearts wrung.

"Mother, I must see her, I must. Once, once only, I won't ask for more. Go after her; go after her. Tell her I love her, I love her always. She will not refuse to see me once—before—before I die!"

Mabin waited no longer. Rushing between the mother and son, she panted out:

"I will go. I will fetch her! I will bring her back. And she will come! Oh, she will come! She is not hard. Trust me, trust me, she will come—she *shall* come."

She gave him no time for more than a hoarse whisper of thanks, and a murmured blessing. She was off, down the hill, as if on the wings of the wind.

And as she drew into the black shadow of the trees on the hill, she heard footsteps and a voice behind her:

"Mabin! Mabin! Don't be frightened. Where has she gone, dear? Where has she gone?"

Panting, breathless, not halting a moment as she ran, Mabin whispered, in a low voice which thrilled him:

"Down the hill—this way. Oh, Rudolph! You don't think she's gone to the sea, do you?"

"Don't let us think about it, dear. If anything has happened to her, it is the fault of that old woman's bitter tongue."

"Oh, don't let us talk. Let us hurry on. We may be in time yet."

"We may."

There was little hope in his tone. At the bottom of the road he, slightly in front, hesitated.

"To the left—to the high part of the cliff, by the sea-mark," directed Mabin briefly. "Don't wait for me. I am getting lame again. Run on alone."

So Rudolph ran. And, behind the fir-plantation a little further on, he disappeared from her sight.

Mabin, her lame foot paining her a little, limped on after him with a sinking heart.

CHAPTER XV.
SOME EXPLANATIONS.

MABIN trudged along the chalky, dry road in the fast-gathering darkness, oppressed by fears. What if Rudolph should not be in time. Now it seemed clear to the girl that poor Mrs. Dale had started on that solitary walk in a frenzy of despair, goaded to a mad act by the taunts of Lady Mallyan.

And if he were in time, what would the end of it be? She could not marry her husband's brother, even if she had returned the love he bore her. Yet, since he had asked so piteously for a few words with her, it was impossible to refuse him.

Mabin's warm heart was full of sympathy for them both; for the woman who had erred so grievously, but who had gone through such a bitter repentance: for the man who, whatever his weakness, his indiscretion, had suffered and been constant.

In the mean time, Rudolph had reached the bare stretch of sandy waste which extended along the cliffs beyond the last of the straggling houses. The tide was coming in below, each little wave breaking against the white wall of chalk with a dull roar, followed by a hissing sound as the water retreated among the loose rocks.

Not a living creature was to be seen, although his seaman's eyes saw a long way in the dusk.

The fears which had haunted him as he ran grew stronger. He looked over with a cold sensation of dread at the water beneath the cliff. He listened, and at last he called:

"Mrs. Dale! Are you anywhere about, Mrs. Dale?"

He was conscious that his voice had not the ring of careless heartiness which it was meant to have. And there was no answer.

He had come to a gap, by which carts and horses went down to the shore to bring away sand and seaweed. A dark object, half hidden in a cranny of the chalk, met his eye. He ran down, and as he approached the thing sprang up and started away from him. But he gave chase, came up with the flying figure as it reached the edge of the water, and caught at the black draperies as he ran.

The long black veil gave way, and remained a limp rag in his hand. But the flying figure stopped.

"Why do you come? Why can't you leave me alone?" she asked fiercely.

And as she turned upon him, he saw in her large, blue eyes, which looked dark and unnaturally bright in the dusk, something of the passionate temper which she had learned by sad experience to control.

Rudolph hesitated. There was a doubt in his mind which made him choose his words.

"He wants to see you, he says he must see you," he said at last, in a low voice. "He told Lady Mallyan so. You cannot, you will not refuse to come."

But a sudden change to terror came over her beautiful face. To Rudolph's great perplexity and distress, she burst into a violent fit of crying.

"I can't go, I can't see him. After what she said! I can't. I would rather die!" Rudolph did not know what to say. His vague and awkward attempts to comfort her were quite without effect, and at last he contented himself by waiting in impatient silence, for the arrival of Mabin. As he expected, the young girl found them out quickly, guided by the piteous sobs of Mrs. Dale.

"Don't cry so, dear, don't cry. The old woman will never dare to worry you again," were the words which Mabin whispered into the ears of the weeping woman, as she threw her arms round her, and at once began to try to drag her up the slope toward home. "She's ashamed of herself already. And you will not have to meet her alone. Remember that."

Under the influence of her gentle words, and still more persuasive caresses, Mrs. Dale speedily became calmer. And although she at first resisted all her friend's efforts to lead her back toward the house she had left, she presently listened to and began to answer Mabin's words.

"I will come with you a little way," she said in a tremulous voice. "You are a sweet, dear girl, and I love you for your goodness. But you must let me go to the station, and get away."

Mabin paused before trying her final shot.

"You must come, dear," she whispered, "because there is some one who wants to see you; some one who is not strong enough to come after you himself."

At these words Mrs. Dale, who had begun to walk slowly up the hill, leaning on Mabin's arm, stopped short and began to tremble violently.

"Who—is—that?" she asked hoarsely, with apparent effort, keeping her eyes fixed on those of her companion with such searching intentness that the young girl was alarmed.

"Mr. Banks," whispered the girl. "And listen, dear. He only wants to see you just once; he said so. And he is ill, you know, so I think you ought. And since he has loved you all this time——"

Mabin stopped short. For as she uttered these words a cry escaped from Mrs. Dale's lips, a cry so full of poignant feeling, so plaintive, so touching, that it was evident she was moved to the inmost depths of her nature.

Clinging to Mabin with trembling fingers, gazing into her eyes with her own full of tears, she said in a low, broken voice:

"He said that? He—really—said—that?"

"Why, yes, he did," answered the girl, not knowing whether to be glad or sorry that the admission had escaped her.

Not another word was uttered by either of them; but Mrs. Dale began to walk so fast that Mabin, whose ankle had not yet recovered all its own strength, found great difficulty in keeping up with her, and Rudolph, who had been ahead of them, had now to drop behind.

It was not until they reached the hill on the top of which "The Towers" stood, that Mrs. Dale's steps slackened, and her face become again overclouded with doubt and fear.

"Is—she with him? Was she with him when you came away?" she asked in a meek and plaintive little voice.

Mabin had to confess that the dreaded "she" had been with him.

And Mrs. Dale faltered again, and had to be further helped and further encouraged. At last, however, the top of the hill was reached, and "The Towers" came in sight.

But the place seemed to be deserted. No one was at the gates; there was no light at any of the windows. A sense of desolation crept into the hearts of both the ladies as they made their way, with slower steps, toward the house. Rudolph hastened forward to open the gate for them. He went through into the garden, and came out again quickly.

"Mabin," he said then, putting his hand lightly on her arm, "let Mrs. Dale go in. I want to speak to you."

Mabin hesitated, for Mrs. Dale was clinging to her arm with an almost convulsive pressure. And then the girl saw that within the garden gates, looking deadly pale in the light of the newly risen moon, "Mr. Banks" was standing. As Mabin disengaged herself from her companion, he came forward, almost staggering, and held out his arms.

"Dorothy! Dorothy!" he whispered hoarsely.

Mrs. Dale uttered a sound like a deep sigh. Then she made one step toward him. But as he approached her, with a pathetic look of love, of yearning in his eyes, she tottered, and would have fallen to the ground if he had not caught her.

Then, reaching Mabin's astonished ears quite distinctly, as she stood, anxious, bewildered, at a little distance, came these words in Mrs. Dale's voice:

"Oh, have you forgiven me? Will you ever forgive me, Geoffrey! Geoffrey!"

Mabin swung round on her feet and all but fell into Rudolph's arms.

"Then—Mr. Banks—is her *husband*!" she gasped, in such a whirl of joyous excitement that she did not notice how unduly gracious to Rudolph her excitement was making her.

"Yes. Didn't you guess?"

"N-n-no. Did you?"

"Yes."

"She didn't tell you then?"

"No. She didn't know herself, I am sure. But she began to wonder and to suspect. And yet she didn't dare, not knowing, I suppose, poor little woman, how he felt toward her, to meet him. So she did the worst thing possible, and sent for his mother. And no doubt the old woman made more mischief, told her Sir Geoffrey would never forgive her, and all that. So the little woman went off her head very nearly. And goodness knows what would have happened if we hadn't gone after her so soon."

Mabin wrenched herself away from Rudolph, who had held one arm round her while he spoke.

"Then that wicked old woman has been cheating her into thinking she killed him, while all the while he was alive and well?" she cried, only now awakening to the full sense of the situation.

"Yes."

"And poor Mrs. Dale has been allowed to torture herself for nothing?"

"Well, it wasn't exactly nothing. She *might* have killed him. Indeed she meant——"

But Mabin would not let him finish.

"Nonsense," she said sharply. "I'm going in by the kitchen-garden. Good-night."

And she fled so precipitately that Rudolph had no time for another word.

In the long drawing-room, no longer a dreary and desolate place, husband and wife were sitting together. Almost without a word she had led him into the house, and, shuddering in the midst of her thankfulness at the sight of the open door of the dining-room, where old Lady Mallyan had shown her so little mercy as to drive her to despair, she had thrown open the door of the drawing-room, where a lamp had been placed upon the table, making a tiny oasis of light in a great wilderness of shadow.

Very gently, very humbly, with eyes still wet, hands still tremulous, she led him to a chair and took her own seat modestly on a footstool near his feet.

"And now tell me," she began in a low voice, as soon as he was seated, "why did you let me think I—I——"

She could not go on.

"My dear child," said Sir Geoffrey tenderly, as he drew her half-reluctant hands into his, and stroked her bright hair, "we have all made mistakes in this unhappy business, and that was the first, the greatest of all."

"It was not your doing, I am sure of that," said Dorothy quickly. "You would not have thought of doing anything so cruel, of your own accord."

He frowned. It had already become clear to him that, in yielding so much as he had done to the advice of his mother, he had not only imperilled his own happiness, but had caused his young wife suffering more bitter than he had imagined possible.

"I was wrong too. I should have known; I should have trusted you more," said he in a remorseful voice. "But you were such a child, you seemed such a feather-headed little thing, I could only believe my mother's judgment when she gave me advice about you."

"But you should not have mistrusted me, however much she said. You should have watched me yourself if you thought I wanted watching."

"I know—I know. I am sorry, child."

"Then why, when I had done the dreadful thing—" and suddenly the fair head bent down in humility and shame—"why didn't you see me? Why didn't you let me see you? And why, oh, why did you let them tell me I had k-killed you? Think of it! Think of it! The horror of that thought is something you can never imagine, never understand."

"When my mother first told you that," answered Sir Geoffrey gravely, "she thought it was true. I was very ill, you know, long after they had extracted the bullet. I was too ill to see you, even if she had let me. And when you had been sent away, I suppose my mother meant to punish you by letting you think as she did."

"Ah, but it was brutal to let me believe it so long!"

"I am afraid it was!"

"But you—when you knew—when at last she told you what I had been taught—didn't you see yourself how cruel it was?"

Sir Geoffrey was silent. He did not wish to own to Dorothy, what he was forced to acknowledge to himself, that his mother had deceived him as egregiously as she had his wife; that, in pursuing her own revengeful and selfish ends, she had gone near to wrecking both their lives. But something, some part of her work was bound to become known; and he had reluctantly to see that the intercourse between his wife and his mother could never be anything but strained.

"I had been led to believe," admitted he, "that your hatred of me was so great, your fear of me too, that even the idea that I had died would not affect you long."

She shuddered, and abruptly withdrew her hand from his. "Dorothy, forgive me. I never meant that you should bear the burden so long. When you rebelled, and insisted on going away from the place where my mother had put you, I had been sent abroad for my health. When I came back, you were gone, and my mother told me you were travelling abroad. But I was already hungering for a sight of you, anxious to see you, to find out whether there was really no prospect of reconciliation for us. And as I found my mother unwilling to help me, I went away, but not abroad as she thought. I had found out where you were, and I determined to settle down near you, and to keep watch for an opportunity of approaching you, and finding out that one thing which was more important than anything else in life to me—whether my young wife was ready to forgive her old husband, and to welcome him back to life."

At these words he paused. Dorothy, her face glowing with deep feeling, went down on her knees and lifted her swimming eyes to his.

"If you could have known—If you could have looked into my heart!" she whispered.

"Ah! my darling, how could I know? I used to watch you from the lane, waiting for hours for what glimpse I could catch of your face through the trees. Then one night, when I was prowling about the place, thinking of you, it came into my head that if I could look on your face while you slept, and call to you, I might speak to you while you were half awake, and tell you what was in my heart and prepare you for finding out that I was alive. So I climbed up to your window, and looked in."

"Ah! That was what I thought was a dream! I saw you!"

"Yes. You were not asleep. You looked at me with such a stare of horror and alarm, that I was afraid of the effect of my own act, and I dropped down to the ground. But some one looked out from an upper window—it was your housemaid, Annie; the next day I met her, and, seeing that she recognized me as the person she had seen the night before, I told her who I was. Fortunately, she had seen my portrait hanging in a room of the house, a locked room, she told me; so that she was ready to believe me."

"Ah!" cried Dorothy.

"And this knowledge that you kept my portrait gave me hope. The girl promised to get me the key of the room in which it was hung, and to leave a window open by which I could get into the house that night."

Dorothy looked up with rather wide eyes.

"These sentimental girls!" exclaimed she. "Supposing you had not been my husband!"

Sir Geoffrey smiled.

"We need not trouble our heads about that now," said he. "I got in that night, but you had played a trick upon me, for in your room there was another lady!"

Dorothy stared.

"Did she see you? Did Mabin see you?" she asked breathlessly.

"She not only saw me. She gave chase, and nearly caught me! I was covered with confusion. But since then the young lady, who is a very charming one, and I have come to an explanation."

"Mabin! And she never told me! Oh, yes she did—I remember. She told me you had promised never to see me again."

And Dorothy, with a little shiver, drew nearer to her husband, and let his sheltering arms close round her.

Rudolph was hanging about the place at an early hour next morning. He sprang upon Mabin as soon as she stepped into the garden, with a particularly happy look on her young face.

"I've come to ask for an explanation," said he, standing very erect, and speaking in a solemn tone, tempered by fierceness.

"An explanation? Of what?"

"Various points in your conduct."

"Oh!" cried Mabin, turning quickly to face her accuser, and evidently ready with counter accusations.

"In the first place, why have you been so cool to me lately?"

"Because—because—was I cool?"

"Were you cool! Yes, you were, and I know why. You were jealous."

Mabin said nothing.

"And now I expect an apology, and an acknowledgment that you are heartily ashamed of yourself."

"Do you expect that, really?"

"Well, I'll alter the form of words, and say that I ought to get it."

"Well, you won't."

"I thought as much. But I am willing to compound for a promise that you will never be so foolish again. There! That's downright magnanimous, isn't it?"

Mabin shook her head.

"I won't promise," said she. "It's too risky."

"You haven't much faith in me then?"

"I haven't much faith in—myself. If I were to see you again apparently absorbed in a very beautiful woman and her misfortunes, I should feel the same again. Especially a widow!"

"But Mrs. Dale was not a widow!"

"Well, a married woman. They are more dangerous than the unmarried ones."

"Well, then if you become a married woman yourself, you will be able to meet them on their own ground. There's something in that, isn't there?"

And although Mabin was astonished and rather alarmed by the suggestion, he argued her into consent to his proposal that he should write to Mr. Rose that very day.

It was astonishing how quickly the neighbors got over their prejudices against the color of "Mrs. Dale's" hair when they discovered that the lady in black was the wife of Sir Geoffrey Mallyan. And although odd stories got whispered about as to the reason for her stay in Stone under an assumed name, it was in the nature of things as they go in the country, where each head weaves its own fancy, that the truth never got known there.

Before the newly united couple left "The Towers," they were both present at the wedding of Rudolph and Mabin, who were married by the Vicar, under the offended eyes of Mrs. Bonnington. Indeed it is doubtful whether she would ever have consented to the marriage, if the accident to Mabin's ankle, although it left no worse effects, had not made it impossible for her ever to ride a bicycle again.

And then, very quietly, and without warning Sir Geoffrey and his wife Dorothy went away, telling nobody where they were going. There was a breach now between them and old Lady Mallyan which could never be entirely healed. But in order that they might have a little time to themselves before they even pretended to forgive her, husband and wife went off to Wales together. And under the tender care of his wife, Sir Geoffrey began quickly to recover the health, the loss of which Dorothy remorsefully traced to the mad act of which she had so bitterly repented.

www.ingramcontent.com/pod-product-compliance
Lightning Source LLC
Chambersburg PA
CBHW011437170626
46808CB00009B/3084